# CURSED MAGIC

## LUNA PIERCE

# Cursed Magic

## HARPER SHADOW ACADEMY: BOOK TWO

### LUNA PIERCE

Alt Book Cover Design by EmCat Designs
Book Cover Design by Mibl Art
Editing by https://studioenp.com
Formatted by EmCat Designs
Editing by Cruel Ink Editing
Proofing by Tiffany Hernandez
First Edition 2020
ISBN 978-1-7332322-4-1 (paperback)
*ISBN 978-1-957238-13-5 (alt paperback)*
ASIN B08BPKJY8J (ebook)

*To anyone struggling, don't give up.*

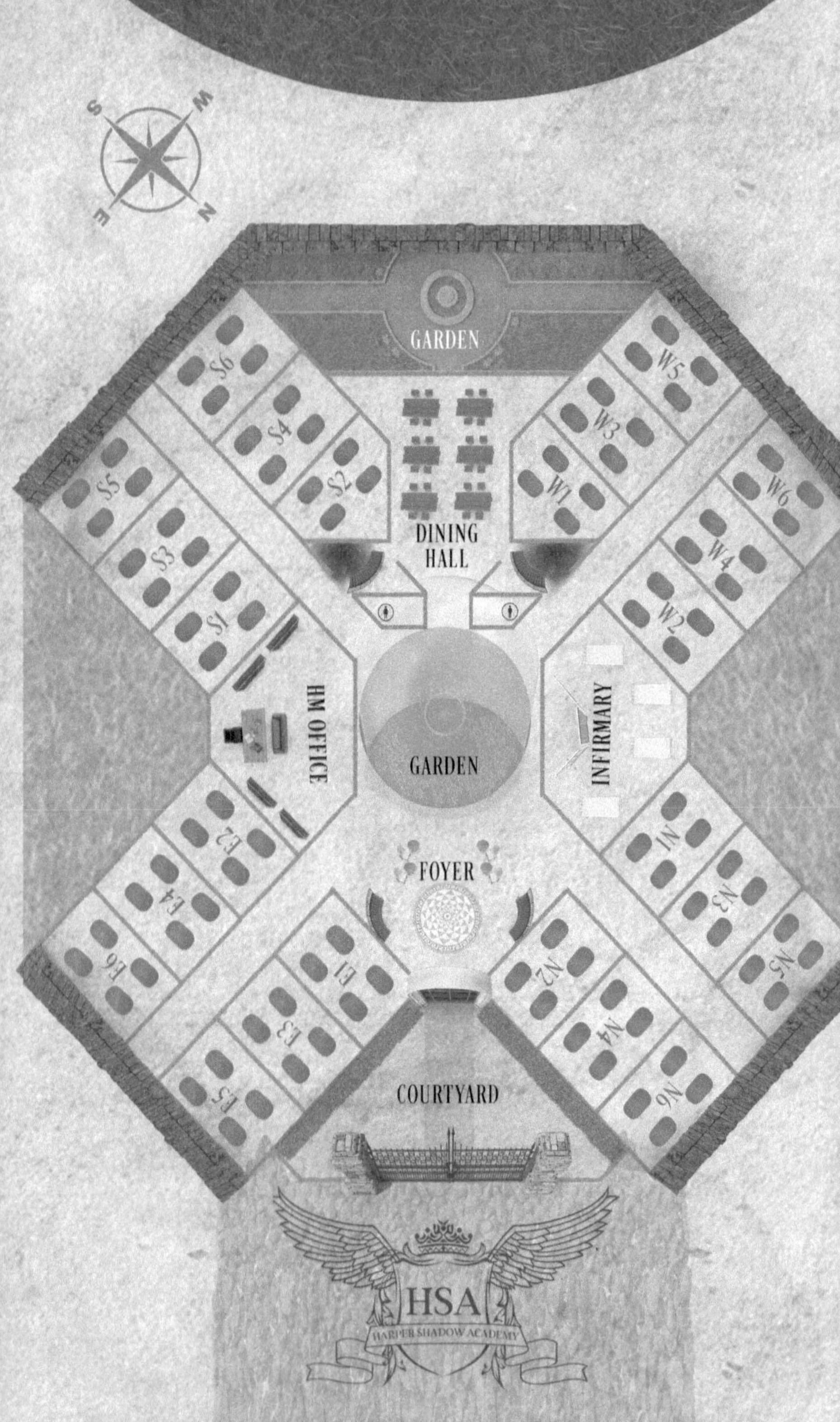

S
W
E
N
GARDEN
S6
S4
S2
S5
S3
S1
W5
W3
W1
W6
W4
W2
DINING HALL
HM OFFICE
GARDEN
INFIRMARY
N1
N3
N5
FOYER
E2
E4
E6
E1
E3
E5
N2
N4
N6
COURTYARD
HSA
HARPER SHADOW ACADEMY

# Basement/ Library

# CHAPTER 1

If someone would have told me a few short months ago that I'd discover I was a witch, a powerful and cursed one, I'd still never be prepared for the insanity that this *new* life brings.

And now, having this knowledge, I have no idea where to start to make sense of it all.

I need to talk to my mom, tell her I've broken the curse—the first one, at least. And find out whatever information she's capable of giving me about our magical bloodline.

I need to explore the library with Abigail and dive deep into the old texts she's been kind enough to help me locate.

I need to give my friends their stolen memories and what little explanation I can to piece together the last few weeks. I miss Remi, Kyra, and Lillian something fierce.

I need to continue making amends with the guys and reiterate how sorry I am for abandoning them the way I did. It was unfair, cruel, and brutal for all of us.

I honestly need to breathe, too. Everything that's happened is a whirlwind of chaos in my head, and it's becoming difficult to ground myself. Not to mention there's a shadow realm in need of repair and some nagging homework that must be completed.

Simply trying to wrap my head around the fact that I'm a witch is a lot to handle.

And there's the whole werewolf, vampire, and demon thing.

It's going to take some time to figure out who I am and how I fit into this world.

"You okay, Willow?" Sydney asks.

I blink away my thoughts. "Yeah, what's up?"

"You've been staring at the wall for a while. Your coffee is getting cold." He nods toward the cup in my hand.

"Oh, right." I shake my head and take a swig of the sort-of-warm latte. Hazelnut today, thanks to barista Sydney.

"No one is rushing you. We can go see your mom another day." His words are kind and delicate, like I'm a fragile being in need of extra care.

"No, it's okay. I'm good. Today is great," I lie with a smile.

A demon invaded our school and tried to kill Cameron and the rest of us—there is no time to wait for the next threat to appear. If I can't protect them, then I need to stay on top of whatever the hell is coming next.

"I can't believe you're leaving us," Cameron calls from down the hall.

My heart warms and breaks at the same moment. "I'll be right back."

Deghan trails beside Cam, and Silas follows behind, keeping his typical distance.

Having them all in the same vicinity, the energy changes and pulses through me. It's heaven on earth.

But with the realization that I hurt them, and that I could do it again, whether or not I mean to, kills the mood immediately.

Silas leans against the far wall, studying me while I study him. With his arms crossed, his black leather jacket bunches and his matching black tee hugs his torso. Dark-gray eyes with a hint of purple, chiseled jawline, always serious expression. He's fucking seductive.

"Gimme a hug." Deghan pulls me in without letting me protest. He smells of honey and cedar. "Be safe. And that's an order, not a request."

I smile into him, hugging him in return. "Okay."

"We won't be long," Sydney confirms. "Walker is only allowing an hour."

Something I'm grateful for but also disappointed about.

Now that a demon broke into the school through the hole I somehow created in the shadow realm, he's pretty much got Harper Academy on lockdown for supernaturals. He enforced extra wards to protect from any other unwanted visitors, but that means the supernatural students can't go to and from whenever they please. He sanctions who comes in and out, and I'm surprised he's letting us go on this adventure today at all.

But, not allowing him the time to change his mind, Sydney volunteered to drive me, and here we are, ready to leave. With a final glance around the room, we head out.

It's a short drive to my house, and this time, Sydney makes all the turns without me telling him.

"If I'm not mistaken, your mom should probably have her magic back, right?" Sydney looks from the road to me, and then back.

I shrug, "In theory. Who's to say that whatever the next curse is, hasn't already suppressed her magic, though?"

"True."

"I'll wait in the car again; I don't want to overstep any boundaries or impose."

"Thanks, Sydney. Maybe when we get some more time, you can meet her."

The car comes to a stop in the drive, and I'm let down by the sight of Danny's vehicle. I was hoping he would be away from the house so I could talk to Mom more privately.

I make my way into the house and find her cleaning the living room.

She's dancing, her body swaying side to side delicately, and I desperately wish I'd snuck in quieter so as to not disturb her. She seems...happy. Her eyes lock onto mine, and she beams.

"Willow, you're home!"

"Hi, Mom."

She embraces me tightly, and a new energy fizzles between us. *Magic.*

I lead her into the kitchen.

"Willow, your hair," Mom says suddenly, brows raising in response.

I coil the strange dark lock around my finger. "Right? It just... happened."

"What did you do? How is this possible?" Her gaze scans my body, like she's looking frantically for something else out of place.

"I didn't dye it, Mom. It literally appeared."

"Yes." She swallows and nods. "It's...honey...it's a sign of dark magic."

"Dark magic?" I mumble, sitting on the chair at the kitchen table.

"Yes, it's a sporadic trait passed through the Oliver witches. Those with silver hair, they're known to be more powerful than the rest, and if they dabble in the darkness, it marks them by turning their hair." She twirls the strand. "This exact way."

"Mom, I...had no idea." The realization settles over me. "It must have been when I took on the demon. I didn't know what I was doing. I felt a rage so fierce. I summoned every ounce of my strength and apparently shattered the shadow realm in the process. Sydney told me he'd never seen that kind of magic."

"Okay, hold on. What are you talking about? Let's rewind a little, tell me exactly what happened."

I take a deep breath and then explain to her, to the best of my ability, what went down at the school. The shadow realm, the supernatural students, the demon who lured Cameron in and used him for bait. It takes up more time than I anticipated, but when I finally finish, a silence falls on the room.

"You...you broke the curse?" she stutters.

"The moment I killed Silas, or at least I thought I did, it must have broken it."

Tears well in her eyes. "Willow, do you realize what this means?" Her voice is merely a whisper.

I shake my head, unsure how to read the implication of her words and her emotions flooding into the space.

"Your father," she breathes. "We can finally get your father back."

My heart thuds loudly. *My father?* A man I had no idea whether or not even existed.

"We have to find him." She grabs on to my arm, squeezing it with almost too much force. "You have no idea what you've done, Willow. I'll never be able to thank you enough. I should have known you'd rid us of this curse."

Little does she know, it's not only one curse, yet many more, and there is no solid information on how many, and what kind, or how to break them. I ultimately have to deal with them one at a time and use my resources to save us from whatever they have in store. *Whoever they may be.* But for now, I have to learn more about how to find this mystery father of mine.

"Mom, please tell me what you know of the curse?"

She inhales deeply. "Tea? We should have tea. Yeah, I'll make some." She stands from her chair and fills a kettle. "So, a long time ago, many generations back, there was some kind of conflict between two covens. Ours and another. The details are sparse, but from what I remember, the Oliver witches were cursed, their magic suppressed and taken, harvested, and used by the other coven. We operate so heavily on love, that in order to take our powers, they stole our love. The heartbreak alone wrecks us so intensely that it binds our magic and makes it easy to steal.

"I was naïve to think it wouldn't happen to me. I fell madly in love with your father, and all too soon, the curse ensued. It drove him mad. It wasn't long after I found out I was pregnant that he left, not because he wanted to, but because he had to. It tore me apart. I had you to worry about, though, honey, so I let him go. I let my magic go with him, and I focused on us. But losing them both, I lost pieces of me that I can't really explain. It's like part of my consciousness was taken. I did my best to put it all behind us, up until that day in the garden. Oh, sweet Willow, you held out your hand, and a flower glowed in your palm. I knew at that moment that your magic had come in and the curse would all start again. I tried to warn you, but it came out in a jumble, it always did, and I wasn't sure if that was part of the curse or not."

I allow the words to sink in and do my best to process them.

"This has to be a lot to take in right now, but you did something incredible, Willow." She holds her hand forward, and an orange glow radiates. "I wasn't sure. I thought something was playing another trick on my mind. It's come in little bursts, but I could feel it pushing its way in. You gave me my magic back." Tears fill her eyes. "And if what you're saying is true, you might have given me my love back, too."

"You never talked about him," I whisper as my heart wrenches.

"It hurt too much. I'm so sorry I never explained what happened."

"But we can find him?" The words come out in a rush.

"I hope so."

"Me, too."

One thing following the next, I'm assaulted by new information. I'm not sure which is the most startling of all. I'm a witch, and while that's mind-blowing, I have a father out there somewhere. There are so many problems that keep bubbling up to the surface, and I have no idea how to fix any of them.

A knock permeates through the front room, my gaze meeting the rickety old screen door. Sydney waves and taps his wrist to indicate the time.

*Shit.*

"Mom, I have to go for now. I'll be back soon, okay? Tell Danny I said hi, wherever he is."

"He's still in bed. He sleeps in late on his days off."

I pull her in for another hug. "Mom, please be careful. And try to answer your phone from time to time. We aren't sure what we're up against." I don't want to burden her with the next words that come out of my mouth, but it's not right to withhold information that could put her in danger. "That curse wasn't the last of them, there are more put into place. I need you to be safe but I'm going to be working every day to figure this out. I promise."

She hugs me tighter, and her magic thrums delicately against me. "I believe in you. You be safe, too." She motions toward the door, toward Sydney.

Once outside, he says, "Sorry, I didn't want to rush you, but we're getting close on time. How did it go?"

I settle into the passenger seat and blow out a huge breath, laying my head back. "I have a dad, and I need to find him."

# CHAPTER 2

We arrive at the school to find Headmaster Walker and Abigail waiting near the entrance.

She waves her arm and flips her wrist, mumbling an incantation, allowing us entry to the grounds.

"What can I do to help?" Sydney parks the car.

I sigh. "I'm not sure. I have no information on him. No name. No idea what color his hair is, his eyes, or his appearance at all."

"We'll figure it out, okay?" He places his hand on top of mine, his attempt to comfort me only working minimally.

"Yeah."

I desperately want to find my dad, to reunite my mom and him, and finally get the chance to meet this mystery man, but then there's this curse threatening to harm everyone I love that I need to focus on. I can't be selfish with so many lives at risk. I have to convince myself to stay on task. Concentrate on the problem with the biggest danger.

The Oliver curse.

"What's next?" Sydney asks.

"The girls, and then the library. I can't think straight, having stolen their memories." And maybe I am being greedy now, but they never deserved what I did to them. At least this way, they can make their own decisions about me without my interference.

His cool green eyes meet mine, and I swallow the lump forming in my throat.

Thick brown hair falls sideways onto his forehead and his energy thrums from his hand into mine. There's sweetness with a hint of something else, something chilling.

We exit the car and head into the school. Once we're inside, I lock my sights on the girls in the dining hall, and I recognize this is my chance to make amends. Quickly, I go straight to the south wing stairs, passing the lush garden and leaving Sydney behind. I jog up the stairs and hesitate in front of my old dorm. Hand in my pocket, I scan the hallway and then click myself invisible.

I knock on the door lightly, and when no one answers, I slip inside unnoticed. I breathe in the scent of the room. Kyra's floral perfume mixed with Remi's potent hairspray and a dash of Lillian's vanilla body wash. My gaze settles on the lone empty bed in the corner. The sight surprises me, given the bed I chose was prime real estate. I sort of assumed one of them would have relocated upon my disappearance.

In a hurry, I say the incantation I memorized by each of their beds. One by one, I relinquish their memories and make my way to my bed, taking the folded sheet of paper from my back pocket and laying it on the pathetic mattress.

The *official* documentation of my transfer to the north wing dorm. My excuse for leaving them, for the change in my schedule. The only thing I have no explanation for is making no effort to see them once I moved, and that will hurt them the most. But, if that's the price I have to pay, I'm willing to do what it takes to have them remember me and the moments we shared, even if it was a short time. Those girls meant, and still mean, so much to me.

I hope they can forgive me, but it's not something I expect. Maybe with time I can make it up to them and help them realize how important they are to me.

I do one last glance around the room and then leave, making sure to creep out as unseen as my arrival. Needing to grab a few things from my room, I go straight there and do exactly that.

I'm stuffing a notebook into my backpack when a knock infiltrates my space. It's loud and urgent, and I can only assume it's one of my guys verifying I'm okay.

Deghan is probably ready for a nap, but he's going to learn how to ration them, considering how many problems I have that need fixing. Despite desperately loving the moments with Deghan, I don't have time for random siestas anymore.

I open the door and am nearly assaulted.

Remi barrels in, pulling me in for a massive hug. "What the hell, Willow?"

Kyra follows her in, and Lillian closes the door behind her.

"You're telling me they gave you *this* room?" Kyra puts her hands on her hips in a purely Kyra style. "Do you have your own bathroom?" Her eyes go wide.

Remi jerks her head toward the corner. "Totally unfair."

Lillian appears the most hurt of all, not really saying or doing anything.

I test the waters. "Hey, Lills."

"Willow." She shifts her gaze away from me.

Willow, instead of Wills. She's pissed.

"Are you serious? You have this place to yourself, and a bathroom? How did you get so lucky?" Kyra continues to scan the room.

Remi smacks Kyra on the arm. "Lucky? She's in here all alone. It's kind of sad. No offense, Wills. And you're missing out on all this." She motions to herself and Kyra and Lillian.

She's not wrong by any means. It may have been my choice to leave them, but it sucks all the same. Yeah, I have a shower to myself, but not having them around the last few weeks has been torture. I should have thought this through more, but at the same time, having magical abilities is sort of hard to hide, especially if you dorm with three non-supes.

"So, what's the scoop?" Remi leans against the wall, crossing her arms. She eyes the bag clutched in my hand. "You going somewhere?"

I follow her gaze. "Uh, yeah. I've been getting some extra help from Abigail."

"Are you failing or something?"

At this, Lillian seems to pay more notice.

"I've had a hard time. It's been difficult to readjust." The words come out, and they're not even a lie. This new life I've found myself living is one struggle followed by another. There are silver linings, like having magic coursing through my body, but there are curses and secrets and demons galore. I didn't expect being a witch to be easy, but I didn't anticipate it would be this hard, either.

"Well then," Kyra chimes in. "Go study. We don't tolerate slackers in our group. But, and I mean a big but, you owe us time carved out in your schedule. Got it?"

Her statement startles me. *They want me around?*

"Really?"

"Are you second-guessing me? Absolutely. You owe us a date. Once a week, preferably more. And I'm demanding that it starts *tonight*. There's a party. Usual spot in the woods. Meet us in our dorm at six to get ready. If you don't show, I'm dragging you from this room. I won't take no for an answer." Kyra's face is solemn with each word.

My heart swells. Never in my wildest dreams did I imagine they'd come for me *this* fast and actually consider hanging out with me. Kyra and Remi seem on board, but Lillian hangs back, not saying anything.

"I'll do my best." I try to measure the energy pulsing through the room, to figure out how Lillian is feeling, but can't seem to get past Kyra's and Remi's.

"Your best is you showing up. Don't let us down, Willow. You owe us." Remi grabs Kyra's arm. "Let's let the lady finish getting ready."

My gaze meets Lillian's, but she turns away and walks out the door.

A bittersweet sensation ensues. Happiness because they care, they still want me in their lives. But sadness from the realization that I've damaged our friendship in a weak attempt to protect them.

Not having time to continue thinking about the situation, I throw my bag over my shoulder and leave my dorm, heading straight down the north wing stairs and through the foyer. I push away the rampant thoughts that fight to have attention solely on them. If stuff continues to happen, I'm going to have to figure out how to clone myself to have a little slack on the considerable to-do list of my life.

*If only that were a real thing.* Trust me, it's not. I checked.

I poke my head into the open door of Headmaster Walker's office and find Abigail reading a book.

"Hey," I call out.

She shuts the text and smiles. "You ready?"

"Ready as I'll ever be."

Abigail seizes her oversized satchel from beside the couch.

My gaze flows across the room to a large mirror. I appear visibly tired, dark circles under my eyes. My hair is tossed in a messy bun, the onyx lock twisted in between pure silver. It's a strange sight, to see my hair anything other than silver. I always wanted it to be some other color, anything but this, but learning that it's caused by using dark magic has me questioning that desire.

Heading out of the office, we're met by an oncoming Cameron.

His dark-blue button-down is undone at the top, and his sleeves are rolled at the bottom. Black jeans and white sneakers pull the rest of the look off well, his golden locks complementing his baby blues. He manages the preppy thing with ease. Damn he's good-looking.

"Hey." He steps in front of us, blocking our path.

"I'll wait over here." Abigail motions to a few feet away.

"What's up, Cam?" I readjust the bag on my shoulder.

"I heard you got a visit from the girls. I take it you did the *thing*?" His gaze shifts around the room, and his voice lowers for the last few words.

I nod. "Mmhm. For the most part, it went well. Lillian seems pissed."

"She needs some time. I'll have Ethan put in a good word." He winks.

"I forgot about him. Are they still an item?"

"They're crazy about each other. It's gross." He shakes his head and laughs.

"That's great." Feeling Abigail's stare, I cut things short. "I've got to get going. Starting the *research* thing with Abby today."

"Of course, yeah. I heard about the girls asking you to the party. Are you going?"

"Word travels fast, doesn't it?" I chuckle and continue, "I don't really have a choice. I think they'll completely disown me if I don't."

"Good." He reaches out and runs a finger down my arm. "Be safe. I'll see you tonight."

"You be careful, too."

His pearly-white teeth show as he smirks and strolls away.

Abigail points toward a stairwell I had no idea existed and takes off in front of me.

"The library was placed down here strategically—given the control of lighting and temperature, it's easier to preserve the integrity of the texts. There are wards to ensure the humidity, and if the school is compromised, the library would be sealed off and protected from outside elements. For example, in the case of a fire. It's quite impressive, the lengths that the academy has put in place to protect them."

We step into a clearing, and I gasp at the shelves stacked from top to bottom lining the walls, and everything in between.

"This is...incredible," I manage.

Round and rectangular tables scatter the floor. Large chairs and comfortable loungers are arranged in the area, too. Only a few people occupy the nearly silent library.

I breathe deeply, the calming scent of old books filling my lungs. I'm brought back to a reassuring time from my childhood, my only friend the endless stacks of books I borrowed from the library. I would spend hours upon hours in my bedroom, reading book after book, occupying my days with fictional places and characters to fill the void in my life. I've always been able to count on them to keep me company, so they became an incredibly important lifeline. I didn't quite understand how much I had been missing them until now, standing in front of this massive collection.

I'm sure I come across as a complete dweeb standing here with my jaw practically dropping in response. To say I'm in awe would be an understatement.

Abigail smiles and tugs my arm. "Oh, you haven't seen anything yet."

# CHAPTER 3

I t takes me a short while to pick my mouth up off the floor. The space Abby brought me to is...for lack of a better word, insane.

At first glance, we walk down a corridor, a lengthy hall that essentially leads to infinite rooms filled with old texts. The walkway is a sort of magical conveyor belt that never seems to end.

Each passing room is filled with a table and chairs, plenty of places to study whatever texts you deem fit.

She explains that the rooms are sorted differently, but it's a hefty chore to figure out how exactly the system works, so it's best to ask an advisor for specific guidance on how to find what you're looking for.

"You'll start to get a hang of it over time, but don't expect it to come quickly."

"It's mind-blowing. How many rooms are there?"

"Hard to tell, really. They keep forming with newly located text. Too many to count."

"How do you keep track of what's in here then?"

"Each book is marked upon its arrival. The master file is aware when the book leaves the library, and then again if it leaves the premises. So long as it's still on the grounds, there are no issues." Her voice has a slight caution to it.

I realize this is a heads-up that I shouldn't take anything off school property.

I hold my hand to my chest. "I wouldn't."

"You'd be surprised at what people will do, Willow." She points ahead to a couple doors to a room. "Ah, here we are."

I peek into a door we're walking past and stop dead in my tracks, doing a double-take. *Silas.*

His head is down, scanning the words on a page in great detail. His presence calls to me and urges me toward him.

Abigail huffs, "He's here often, don't be surprised."

"Really?" I whisper, not wanting to startle him.

He glances up at the same time Abigail grabs my arm and pulls me away.

I ache to stay in place, to be near him.

She enters the spot and holds out her arms. "Here we are." She smiles brightly. "Now, this one is a tad bigger than the rest. Not really sure how that happened, but it's sort of become the prime location for people to study. I've gone ahead and reserved it for the foreseeable future, though."

"That's a thing? Reserving them?" I scan the area, studying the overfilled shelves.

"It's more of a courtesy, really. The supes are often private regarding their own matters, so we try to give each other a warning if we need a specific study. But because this one is a bit popular and off the beaten path, I went ahead and made sure it was yours."

"Thanks, Abby. I don't really need this much room, though.

If anyone else needs this one, I'm happy to share." It doesn't seem right to keep it all for myself.

She places her hand on my shoulder. "Some of the information you seek is in here, Willow. You're entitled to that."

"Really?"

"Yep. This is where I was able to find some of the ancient text about the Oliver's." Her expression saddens. "I'm not guaranteeing you'll find what you need here, but it's a start."

"Wow, okay." I trail my gaze over the tattered and dusty volumes.

"I think I'm going to give you some time to adjust. To wander if you want. Here." She holds out her hand, a small object placed gently in her palm. "It's a beacon. The library can be a tad overwhelming, so this will help you find your room if you need it."

I take the item and flip it over, examining. It's about the size and shape of a quarter, but with an arrow, sort of resembling a compass, that pulses and shines with a green light. "You really think of everything, don't you?"

"I try to." She smirks and pulls a couple of books from her bag. "Here. To get you moving in the right direction. I found some stuff you haven't looked at yet when I tried to do my own research. It's encrypted, though, and it could be a shot in the dark, but your magic might be the key to unlocking it." She nods toward the thing in my hand. "If you need me, hold on to that tight and call out for me. Oh, and another thing, the library is in the same time zone as the school, so don't forget to keep an eye on that. People often lose a whole day down here with no windows."

She leaves me there to gawk at the device and the texts in front of me.

I sigh, looking from one shelf to the next, scanning the contents. The books are nearly indistinguishable, and I'm not really sure how anyone can tell them apart.

A throat clears, and I jump.

"Didn't mean to startle you," Silas says while leaning against the doorframe.

"You didn't, er, well...I guess you did." My tone lightens. "This is all super overwhelming." I motion at the wall.

"Anything I can do to help?"

I swallow, remembering how intense it is to be around him, to touch him, especially now that no invisible forces are disallowing it to happen.

"I'm not really sure where to start."

"Don't let yourself get overwhelmed, otherwise you won't begin at all. Focus on one thing at a time." He steps into the room.

My heart picks up its pace.

He strides to the table, latching onto one of the books that Abigail left behind and then closes the distance between us. He holds it out, and his gaze meets mine. "Here. Baby steps."

His energy pulses through me. Cool and potent and undeniably magnificent.

His hand touches mine, and I find myself unable to function.

The way I feel around him is a lot to handle and sort of makes me feel crazy, because there is no way he feels this, too, right? The pull, the connection, the magnetic attraction.

Silas's face is tense and rigid, his lips a memory away from wrecking me. That potent kiss from the time I tried to tell him goodbye, to put all of the guys in the past and attempt to move on, to give them what I thought they deserved.

That kiss set me over the edge. It was passionate and desperate and everything and nothing I ever could have imagined a first kiss with someone to be. It set me on fire and has left me wanting more and more and more.

"Silas," I mutter, not daring to take my eyes off him. "You said this was fate and a curse wrapped up in one."

His eyes change, a cool gray morphing into a darkness with hints of purple, and he looks away. "Let's not talk about that."

"What, why? I broke the curse, what can you tell me about the fate?"

He shakes his head. "Maybe another time."

I grab on to his arm, not quite in control of my own body or mind, but desperately wanting answers to anything I can find. "Please."

Abigail told me he was fated to one true love, but maybe she was wrong. I want to hear what the Harlow fate is all about, and I want to hear it from him, but I can't exactly force it out of him.

"You have work to do," he says, changing the subject with ease. Poking his finger onto the book in my hand he says, "Good luck."

"You're going to leave me?"

"Not when you say it that way." He exhales. "Can I join you?"

"Of course. I'd love that."

"I'll get my things, but this is strictly business, deal?"

Damn it. I was hoping I could get him to talk. He does have a point, though; I do need to get some work done.

"I'll try my best, but don't hold me to it."

He smirks and leaves the room, only to enter again in a fast second. His vampire speed reminds me of how little knowledge I have about this world.

Silas settles into the chair next to mine, careful not to sit too close but somehow never close enough. Maybe this is a bad idea.

I'm not sure how much work I'll be able to focus on with my mind being glued to him.

I push the thoughts of his decadent lips and mesmerizing eyes, his strong arms drawing me and daring me to run my hands along them.

I open the book he handed me, and all the images in my mind disappear, replacing them with an intricate puzzle. I can't quite understand why or how, but my gaze trails an outline on the page, up and down and side to side, up again, and over and over until *bam*, a burst of energy pops from the page and fizzles out in the room.

"What the hell was that?" I mutter on a gasping breath.

"I heard Abigail mention she couldn't decipher the text. I think you unlocked it, Willow."

"I did?" How is that possible? How did I do that? Did he know that was possible when he handed me this book?

"You're incredibly powerful, more so than you're aware."

I look to him, scanning his face for something, validation perhaps.

He appears happy, proud even.

As much as it pleases me to hear these things and see him the way he is right now, it terrifies me all the same. I have no real control over my magic, or any information about how it came to me, and why I'm so powerful. Especially considering I broke an ancient curse that no other Oliver witch was able to. Why me? With this power must come great evil, and I have no idea if I'm capable of handling what's coming for me.

"What's wrong?" His eyebrows furrow.

I shift my gaze to the text. "I'm scared," I admit in disbelief at the words actually coming out of my mouth. I glance back at him. "That must make me a coward."

Silas blinks slowly, his expression loosening. He scoots toward me, tugging at my shoulder to reel me in for a hug. "No, you're not a coward, Willow."

He pats my head, and I pull away slightly.

"You don't have to lie to me."

He puts his finger under my chin, tilting my head up to meet his gaze. "I wouldn't lie to you, not now, not ever. You don't have to believe me but you're more courageous than anyone I've encountered." He trails his finger along my cheekbone, leaving a trace of heaven in its wake. "You're going to do great things, you already have. Don't doubt yourself."

"How can you be so sure?" My voice is barely a whisper.

He leans forward, his breath against mine, his lips lingering. "Because you gave us this." He presses them onto the corner of my mouth and kisses me so gently, it's like he's afraid I'll break in two. He pulls away without letting me react.

"Tell me you feel this, too," I say, out of breath.

"I've felt it since the day you stepped foot on the school's property. Not to mention before and after. It only grows and gets stronger." He shifts back into his seat.

Is he ashamed of his declaration?

"What's stopping you?"

He looks away, at the door, and for a second I'm afraid he'll bolt.

"I'm scared, too."

"Scared of what?"

"You."

Me? What could he possibly be afraid of me for? Is it because I'm *powerful* and he thinks I'll hurt him, the same thing I was worried of not too long ago? I shut all of the guys out because I didn't want to put them in danger, and maybe I was selfish for letting them back in. I keep being torn between not fully understanding whether I'm doing the right or wrong thing by keeping them around. Maybe until I get a grip on my curse I should keep them at a distance, despite every bit of my heart compelling me that's the wrong thing to do.

Will I ever be sure of whether or not what I'm doing is a mistake? I nearly cost Cameron his life, and I killed Silas. Yeah, he's a vampire but what if he wasn't? How could I live with myself knowing I did that?

I'm a monster. And maybe Silas has finally figured that out.

# CHAPTER 4

Seeming to sense the hurt in my voice, Silas immediately says, "Willow, I'm not scared of you in *that* way."

"How then? I killed you. I snapped the bones in your body and watched you fall to the floor, lifeless. You're worried I'll use my *powerful* witch juju and kill you for real." My voice shakes on every word.

"No, I mean, don't get me wrong, you're strong as hell, but I'm not worried in that sense. I'm afraid of you killing me in another way...by breaking my heart." He shifts and avoids eye contact.

*Oh.* I'm a fool, I really thought he was *afraid* of what I'm capable of doing with my magic. Never did I ever consider he'd feel this way.

"I don't want to hurt you in any way, ever."

He manages a weak smile. "I hate admitting any of this. I've never spoken to anyone in this capacity, and it's...it's all I can do to not run out the door."

"Thank you for staying."

"I've lived a long time, Willow. Never did I imagine I'd find *you*. And now that I have, the thought of losing you is almost too much to bear. I can't picture a life without you in it."

"I feel it, too."

"I've never been so...vulnerable. And I'm not sure how to handle that. It's like a sensory overload, nothing I've ever experienced." He fidgets with his hands underneath the table.

I press mine to his shoulder, willing him to be at ease. "You can let your guard down with me. I'm sorry I left the way I did. I pushed you away and I'm sorry, but never will I ever hurt you on purpose. I promise you that, Silas." I force the calming magic out of me without realizing it, noticing his face shifting in the process.

"How did you do that?" he asks suddenly.

I shrug. "It's one of those things I can do. I'm sorry if it was out of line. I hate *feeling* you feel that way. I want the best for you."

"That was incredible. I still have the thoughts of being afraid, but you got rid of the physical manifestation of it." He beams. "You're brilliant, truly."

"You give me too much credit." I nudge him.

"Okay, enough uncomfortable talk for the day. Let's get to work." He points at the book in front of me, dying to be read.

---

Hours go by with no progress. I pace around the room with the text in my hand, scanning the pages trying to make sense of the words. Sure, I unlocked it, but I have no idea how to read this old language. Everything is written in code—short snippets that don't make any sense on their own.

I scan the page and flip to the next with no luck. Whoever

wrote these was either a genius or a complete idiot. I can't help but feel the latter trying to figure it out.

I snap the book shut and dust flies up and out.

"No luck?" Silas asks.

"It's like someone's playing a trick on me. I have no idea how to read this." I hold out the book and toss it onto the table.

"You have to be patient with this kind of stuff. Trust me. I've been reading the same texts for *decades* and only rarely make any progress."

*Decades?* How old is he?

"How have you not given up then?" I ask, hesitant to shine a light on my other nagging question.

"Determination, I suppose. What good does giving up do? Sure, I wouldn't have to spend time reading and re-reading, but every so often I find something useful, and that makes it all worth the wait." His eyes gleam.

For a second I think he's talking about something other than reading old books.

"You're right. I just found out I'm a witch, I should have some patience with the whole process." I sit onto the table, putting my feet on my chair. "Will you tell me about you?"

"All business, remember?"

"Not about fate, about *you*, and being a vampire. No one has told me what it entails, and I don't really want to make assumptions. Like if you turn into a bat or if I should avoid eating garlic around you or something. Everyone has given me info on a limited basis because of the energy thing, but I want to learn."

He laughs a little, but his energy tells me he's nervous. Vampirism must be a touchy subject.

"Neither of those things are true, although turning into a bat would be cool."

At this, I giggle. "Oh wow. The *infamous* Silas Harlow thinks something is *cool*."

He shakes his head. "You're mocking me!"

"I'm not mocking you; I'm mocking everyone else for how

they see you. They think you're all tough and scary and anti-social. Speaking of which, what's up with Sydney, why do you two really hate each other so much?"

"Sydney...well...witches and vampires typically have a natural disposition against each other. He takes that rather seriously."

"I don't naturally despise you, must be a Sydney thing. What else? You're super-fast and are clearly immortal." And you're beyond gorgeous and incredibly endearing when you want to be. I fold my arms over my chest and wait for his reply.

"You're right with those two. I have increased speed and can live longer than humans, given I don't take a stake to the heart."

He doesn't seem to want to give up any other information willingly.

"What do you...eat?" I ask the question I'm sure he's trying to avoid.

"I can eat people food, but I need blood to survive." He shifts. "Don't get freaked out, though, I'm on a purely animal diet, so don't worry about that."

"And you can heal yourself?"

"Certain things are harder than others, but yeah, vampires heal at a much quicker rate than humans. Werewolves do, too."

*Werewolves. Deghan.*

"Of course, you saw that I had powers, in the shadow realm. All supernatural beings have some kind of *magic*."

"What about the sun?"

He snorts. "The sun does affect us, but not how it does in the movies. It *burns* but won't kill us, not unless we're in direct light for an extended period. We've evolved and taken precautions, though, to eliminate the pain where we can."

"Is that it?" I can't help but think he's not telling me everything.

"Not exactly, but what's the fun in knowing it all?"

"It would be nice to not be so damn clueless all the time."

Silas's face changes, and his shoulders stiffen. He focuses on something else for a second. "Someone is coming."

Fear washes over me but is whooshed away seeing Deghan appear in the doorway, his sturdy, muscular frame filling the space.

"Hey, sorry, didn't mean to interrupt," he says. "But Remi and Kyra are going to have a coronary if you don't get to their room ASAP."

I glance to the clock by the door. *Shit*, I'm going to be late.

"Thanks, Deghan," I say while stacking the books on the table. "I'll be right there."

"Cool, I'll wait for you down the hall." He winks and leaves.

"Where are you going?" Silas asks, and if I had to guess, it wasn't because of jealousy, but more so because he's worried.

"There's a party tonight. The girls invited me and basically said if I want to be friends with them again, I have to go. It's the least I can do, considering what I did to them." I study his face.

"Have fun, but be safe, okay?" His request is sincere.

I smile. "I'm sure you'll be lurking in the shadows."

"Is it that obvious?" He stands from the table and pushes in his chair, and then mine.

"Mmhmm." I nudge him on the way out the door.

He stops in his path, and I turn back.

"You coming?" I ask.

"I'll see you in a little bit. I'm going to hang here for a little longer." He hesitates in the entryway to the room he was in by himself earlier.

Part of me wants to reach out and hug him, but I'm not sure if it's too forward. He did kiss my face not too long ago. Not wanting to make the first move, I hold back.

His gaze settles over me, and a long moment passes. "I'll find you." And then he disappears into the room.

Disappointment weaves through me, and I fight it back, not sure why I expected anything else from the situation anyway. His absence becomes a dull ache at my core with each step away.

Deghan pulls me in and squeezes tightly. "Wills, you've been down here for hours. How did it go?"

"Uh, not the greatest. I unlocked some magical *Oliver* book, but have no idea how to read it, so that's cool." I allow him to guide me down the narrow hallway and into the normal library.

"It happens. You'd be surprised how long it takes people to find out about their lineage. Took me a while, and I haven't learned much." He takes my hand and leads me up the stairs.

"Your parents didn't tell you?" I recall him mentioning his parents the time he told me why he's never missed a sunset, but I don't think he's ever elaborated about them since then.

"Nope. I lost them both as a kid and was raised by my aunt and uncle. Found out about being a werewolf the hard way."

"Oh, Deghan, I'm so sorry."

"Thanks, Willow." He firmly tightens his hand around mine. "Now, if you're anything like me, you've got to be starving after spending all that time down there."

The thought of food sends my stomach growling. "Absolutely."

We enter the dining hall and head toward the food.

I decide on a grilled chicken sandwich, French fries, a tea, and dollop some honey mustard on my plate for dipping.

Deghan fills his tray with two large slices of pizza, a cheese-burger, and a salad. "It's a wolf thing," he whispers.

"I'd say so." If I didn't know any better, I would never assume Deghan had washboard abs hiding under his shirt. But he does, and boy are they chiseled to perfection. Even his biceps strain against the fabric of his sleeves, daring to burst through at any moment. Despite the hard surface, he's so damn cozy, and every single embrace is like a pillow hugging my body.

"You're totally judging me hardcore." He laughs, setting his plate on a nearby table.

"Exact opposite," I admit.

"Ooh, you think I'm dreamyyy." He taps me with his elbow and then dangles his slice of pizza in front of him and takes a bite.

"Don't make me go eat with someone else."

He clutches his chest with a partially full mouth and says, "You wouldn't."

"Don't tempt me." I dip a fry in sauce and shove it in my mouth. Unwrapping my sandwich, I realize I really am near starving.

---

We eat in a rush, not wanting to keep the girls waiting any longer, but not wanting to go through a pretty princess makeover on an empty stomach.

Deghan finishes my remaining fries, and once he's done, he walks me to the south dorm.

The energy is fully different here than in the west and north wing. The amount of juice the supernaturals give off is a lot to get used to. The human dorms are so...normal. The only thing I pick up on here is hormonal young adults stressing over boys and homework.

"You'll be there tonight?" I confirm.

"Wouldn't miss it." Deghan smiles and bumps my chin with his hand. "See you shortly, pretty lady."

*"You're not pretty,"* a voice in my head bellows.

What the hell was that? It sounded so similar to my voice but strained.

The door to the girls' room bursts open, and Remi latches on to my arm, yanking me in with her. "About damn time. I really thought you were going to no-call, no-show."

I rub the spot on my arm when she lets go. "No, I got side-tracked at the library and had to eat first. You don't want to deal with me hangry. But I wouldn't miss this for the world."

"Over there," she demands. "Now, sit."

I sigh knowing I'm in for some old-fashioned makeover torture.

# CHAPTER 5

"There!" Kyra calls out. "You're perfect."

I stand, adjusting the skintight dark-gray tank top hugging my torso, and walk to the mirror.

My silver hair, in subtle beach waves, has that one lock of onyx weaved into a braid on the side. Black lines my eyes, and a hint of pink dusts my lids. I'll never fail to be amazed at the work Remi and Kyra do. They should both consider careers in cosmetology or fashion.

Lillian seems pleased with her transformation, too. A dark-red top complements her well, her hair curled to precision.

"You look beautiful, Lills," I say in a desperate attempt to warm her up.

"Thanks," she replies bleakly.

In the few hours I've been in this room, the heartache over

what I put them through has both been eased and intensified. Remi and Kyra are taking to my quality time with them, but Lillian is hesitant to welcome me back in. And I don't blame her. I would be wary of one of my friends disappearing into thin air. It pains me to not be able to tell her the truth, but I understand that no matter how much I want to, I can't.

Lillian hurts the most, though, considering how close we became in such a short amount of time. She was my rock, my constant, keeping me grounded when I wasn't sure who I could count on. I left her hanging like a complete asshole. It's no surprise she's standoffish. With time, I hope she forgives me, at least enough to be my friend again.

*"She'll never forgive you,"* the voice from earlier calls out.

My stomach sinks. What if it's right?

Remi slides her arm under mine. "Ready?"

"Yep." I force a smile and lean into her. "I missed you girls."

"And we missed you, brat," Kyra chimes in.

"I don't care who changes your schedule, next time, they go through me," Remi says.

We exit the room and head through the south dorm hallway, following each other down the stairs and into the center of the building.

I want to pull Lillian aside and talk to her alone, but it might not be the best time for it. Hopefully, I'll get a chance at some point during the party.

Cameron and Ethan stroll toward us, Ethan immediately gawking at his girl.

"Lill, you look stunning." He grabs her hand and twirls her in a circle.

Her face lights up, and it brings me joy to see her happy with him.

Cam's eyes meet mine, and he grins, coming to my side. He leans in so only I can hear. "You're killing me, Willow."

"What did I do?"

"You know what you did," he teases. "Have you seen you?"

"Oh hush," I respond.

He turns to face me while continuing to walk backward, through the dining hall. "You're absolutely beautiful." He scans me up and down, but not in a demeaning way, more like admiration.

I return the exchange. His light-blue button-down shirt complements his that-much-bluer eyes. His smile grows while he watches me watch him. He runs a hand through his golden hair and flips his body to join me in going the correct way.

"You're not so bad yourself." I wink at him.

The group gains more and more people as we make our way through the doorway, out onto the oversized patio, and onto the grounds behind the school.

Deghan and a few of his friends join in, and I can't help but wonder where Sydney and Silas are. Silas is usually always close by, but I can't locate the pressure of his stare quite yet.

"Sydney's on his way," Deghan tells me like he somehow read my mind.

*"You don't belong here,"* the voice says.

I shake my head to rid myself of whatever nonsensical trick it's playing.

"You all right?" Cam asks, his expression kind as always.

"Yeah." I seize his arm and tug him to me. "This is nice." I breathe him in, reeling in the clean citrusy aroma.

Arriving at the clearing, the guys make quick work of the fire and then tap the keg someone somehow procured.

Cam gets me a water. "Under no circumstance will you drink from anything other than this bottle." He rustles through his pocket and acquires a permanent marker, writing my name on the bottle. "Better safe than sorry. But if this bottle is ever out of your sight, you're not to drink it. Okay?"

"Yes, sir," I reply. "You're on top of things tonight."

"After what I heard of what *really* happened, no way in hell am I letting it happen again. Not on my watch, Miss Oliver."

"So kind of you. Thank you, Cam."

The music comes on, and a group forms near the source, bodies wiggling to the beat. It's not long until Remi grasps my arm, peer pressuring me into the dance area.

I latch onto Deghan on the way.

Cam is already making his trek toward the group, my bottle of water in his back pocket for safekeeping. He really is one of the most thoughtful and considerate people I've ever encountered. And somehow, still, despite being almost killed by a demon and finding out your new best friend is a werewolf and the girl you have a crush on is a witch.

We're dancing our little hearts out when I notice a shift in the energy.

*Silas.*

I keep dancing, taking Remi's hand and twirling her around. If I don't go to him, maybe he'll come to me. But that's a fat chance, considering how he never attends these types of things.

He told me his bloodlust was under control, but what-if it's not and that's why he doesn't come to parties, where booze is flowing and blood is pumping wildly through our veins? What if he *wants* to attend but can't because of that?

The thought halts me, and I lock eyes with Cam, throwing my thumb toward the woods and mouthing, "I'm gonna pee."

He points at himself and squints in response.

"I'll be okay," I call out to him.

Without letting any of the girls see or stop me, I go straight to where the dull ache calls me to. It's like I have my own internal Silas compass, guiding me to him without me really knowing how.

I step through a wooded area and allow my eyes to adjust to the darkness.

A hand wraps around my arm, twirling and pushing me smoothly against a tree.

My lips turn up at the corners. "Hey."

"I warned you it wasn't safe out here," Silas mutters.

"I knew you were here. I wouldn't have come if I didn't."

He steps back, releasing me from the tree. "You *knew*?"

"Mhm."

"How?"

"I just did. Probably the same way you were aware I was in danger. There's some invisible pull between us." I lean onto the large oak.

"I thought only I could feel that." He rubs at his neck.

"Nope, so...dare to tell me what this *fate* thing is all about?"

He huffs. "Not a chance."

"If you won't tell me, how about you come to the party?"

His eyes scan mine, and a long moment passes. "I'm not really a party kind of person."

"Neither am I, but it would make me happy if you came...for a little while." I push the issue to see if it really is because of being a vampire.

"Fine."

He says the word, and my heart jumps. "Really?"

He smiles. "Don't act so surprised, but I'm not staying long."

I leap from the tree and wrap my arms around him, hugging him tight with not a care in the world how intrusive of his boundaries I'm being right now. The energy between us is fierce, calling for more. I don't think I'll ever be close enough to him, and I'll never be able to will myself to stop trying.

He hesitantly wraps his arms around me and relaxes into the embrace.

Now, going to the party seems to be a shit idea. Letting go of him an impossible task.

Silas slides his hands down my waist, gently tugging my hips in an attempt to pry me off him.

*"He doesn't want you,"* the voice calls.

I drop my hands in response, the words a punch to the gut. What is going on inside my head? That can't be true, can it?

"What was that?" Silas asks.

"Nothing." I shake my head.

He cups my face in his hand. "Tell me if something is wrong, please."

"I'm okay." I take his arm. "Let's go." Forcing away the thought, I all but drag him to the clearing. "Look who I found," I announce.

Deghan clasps Silas's shoulder. "What's up, man?"

Silas looks from Deghan, to me, back to Deghan.

I can't tell whether he's shy or simply hates parties.

Angry energy penetrates my chest, and I scan the immediate area. My gaze settles on the cause. *Allie.* The girl I overheard in the shower a few weeks ago who has a crush on Silas. And here I am, flaunting him in front of her. I'd be pissed, too. But at the same time, she has no right. Silas is not her property, and if he wanted to be with her, then he would.

I run my hand in small circles on Silas's back, pushing my calming energy into him. Whatever his aversion to parties, maybe I can help him in the short term.

He tilts his head to the side in acknowledgment of the shift in his energy and shakes his head. "You're one of a kind, Willow." His lips beg me to lean in and press mine to them.

I find myself unable to break my concentration from him. The world seems to slow and it's just me and Silas in this little bubble of bliss.

But it's not, and I realize that the moment a body crashes into mine and I'm drenched with a wickedly cold liquid.

"What the...?" I yelp, stumbling back.

"Oh my god," a dramatic voice says. "I'm so sorry, I should really watch where I'm walking."

I settle my gaze on the culprit. *That bitch, Allie.*

Cameron, Deghan, Silas, and out of nowhere, Sydney, are at my side, the girls filing in around them. Even Lillian joins the group.

Kyra begins to speak, but I cut her off. I don't need her fighting my battles.

"What's your problem, Allie?" I stand my ground, some nasty-smelling drink soaking into my shirt.

She bats her eyes. "It was an accident, don't be so sensitive."

"Accident my ass, I saw you staring at me a minute ago. So what is it?" I take a step toward her, daring her to tell me the truth.

A warm and familiar hand lands on my arm, getting my attention. "We, uh, we need to go," Sydney says.

He points to the mess on my clothes, and it takes me an extra second to register his concern.

She spilled alcohol on me, and now it's seeping into my skin, threatening to weaken and hinder my magic, and my ability to function.

"This isn't over," I say to her and turn on my heel. "I'll find you girls once I've cleaned up," I say to Remi, Kyra, and Lillian. I focus on Lillian, and she nods slightly, giving me more than I expected.

Stomping away from the clearing, I mutter obscenities.

# CHAPTER 6

The guys and I walk the path to the school in silence.

Sydney was right in his concern and it's not long before the effects of the alcohol firmly root itself in place, a weird uneasy feeling resolving over me.

I take a step and wobble. Is it reacting quicker than the last time?

My vision blurs, and my pace slows.

Hands on my neck and under my legs. Lifting me.

*Silas.*

"Sorry," I manage.

*"You're such a burden,"* the evil voice declares.

I wince, the statement searing my heart.

"Hurry," Silas calls out. He rushes us forward and to the

entrance of the school rapidly, only slowing for what I assume are humans in the dining hall.

Reaching into my waistband, I pull out my saving grace. I click the pen and Silas and I go invisible.

The rest of the journey goes by in a flash, Silas using his vamp speed to get us to Sydney's room. He holds me tight against his body. "It's going to be okay," he coos.

"This is bullshit," I reply, making us visible again.

He laughs. "Yeah, it is."

"All because she likes you."

"What?"

"Allie. That's why she's mad."

"She's going to have to get over it. I'm spoken for."

I smile at his words, desperately hoping they mean what I think they do.

*"Not you,"* evil me says.

The rest of the guys barrel up the stairs and into the dorm hallway.

"Damn, Silas, you're fast," Cameron says, out of breath. "Is she okay?"

"She's right here," I joke. "Ready to kick Allie's ass."

"You're not fit to kick anyone's ass, Willow," Sydney teases. "You, get her, I don't want *him* in here."

Deghan shrugs and takes me from Silas.

"I'll be right here," Silas reassures.

I'm placed on a bed in Sydney's room, and he does his witchy stuff, waving his glowing hands and setting a sparkly white crystal on my chest.

It's only a few moments later, but damn do I feel drastically better once he's done his thing.

I sit up, glancing down at my still soaked shirt. *How cute.* "Thanks, Syd, what would I do without you?"

"Willow, I'm not sure how to say this..."

"Say it, please. What's wrong?" Worry consumes me.

"This time, everything happened much quicker. The glitch, it was more potent than last. When I eliminate it from your body, I process it into mine. It *felt* different."

"So, Allie's drink had a higher alcohol content?" My gaze scans the room. "What was everyone drinking?"

Cameron shrugs. "I think it was the usual. Sometimes people sneak in bottles of harder stuff."

"That explains it then, she probably had vodka or something," I say.

"You drank a clear liquid last time, though, right?" Sydney asks.

I recall the memory, grabbing what I thought was my bottle in a quest to drown my thirst with my water. "Yeah, I was convinced it was water."

"Then *that* was probably vodka, *this*, this is something else."

Deghan chimes in. "Are you saying someone purposely put Allie up to pouring that on Willow? In an attempt to weaken her defenses?"

Sydney nods and rubs his chin. "It's very well possible."

The door flies open, Silas standing in the entrance.

Sydney shifts his focus to me. "No more parties. Not until you can learn some protection spells."

"Okay. Can you help me with that?" Or I could ask Abigail for assistance.

"Yeah, but right now, you need to get changed out of those clothes and then come back so I can make sure it doesn't take hold again." He looks between the guys. "Can someone escort her to her room while I recharge?" His green eyes are dull and lack their normal luster.

"We've got it." Cameron grips my hand and helps me stand. "You okay to walk?"

"How are you so good at dealing with all of this?" I ask.

His face scrunches in response. "What do you mean?"

I motion around the room. "All of *this*. Aren't you overwhelmed?"

"Not really. You're all the same people, but with supernatural abilities. If anything, now I don't feel quite so clueless."

Leave it to Cameron to be accepting of the supernatural world. He's a kind soul and such a selfless human.

*"You'll never be good enough,"* the voice screams inside my head.

It's everything I can do not to react.

Walking through the open area, Silas leans in close. "It happened again, didn't it?"

How is he so in tune with me?

I shake my head and play dumb. "What?"

"I'm going to find out what's going on, Willow. Or you could tell me." His bossy possessiveness is adorable and shows me that he cares.

*"He doesn't care about you."*

"There it was. What is that?"

Tears well in my eyes, and I fight them back. Insecurities come flooding in.

Failing, disappointment, rejection, abandonment. They threaten to destroy me.

"Nothing," I lie. "I'm okay." I approach my dorm. "Give me five." I step through, shutting them out and stripping my clothes off immediately. I hop in the bath, scrubbing away the night, the makeup, the alcohol. I take a record-fast shower and dry off even quicker, slapping some lotion on and throwing on a pair of sweatpants and T-shirt. It's not cute, but it serves its purpose. Can't exactly go back to the party now anyway.

A knock rattles the door, and I finish throwing on a pair of cozy socks.

"Willow?" Deghan asks.

"I'm okay. One more second." I swing the door open and note the gawking eyes. "Yeah, yeah. I know, I look like a homeless person now."

Cameron smacks Deghan playfully. "Your jaw." He points to the floor.

"If *this* is what homeless people look like, I'm dropping out of school," Deghan says.

"Enough," Silas commands. "Back to Sydney to confirm she's clear."

I tuck a stray strand of hair behind my ear, blushing at their response.

*"Ugly,"* the voice calls. *"You're nothing."*

Avoiding Silas at all costs, I stride right through Sydney's door, leaving him waiting. It's cruel, especially since he's not wrong, but I can't tell him the details of what's going through my head. I don't understand it, let alone do I want to divulge the intimate vulnerabilities.

I stop in front of Sydney, and he studies me.

He waves his hand over my body, head to toe, muttering something. He finishes and meets my eyes. He's tired, and it shows, dark circles appearing and his lids drooping. This must take a lot out of him. "You're good to go."

"Is there something I can do for you?" I reach out to caress his arm.

"I just need some sleep." He places his hand on mine and weakly smiles. "Tomorrow, though, we'll work on building your barriers to protect you from these types of weaknesses."

I leave his room in hopes that he'll be able to rest. The remaining guys follow me down the hall.

"I told the girls I would find them once I got cleaned up." I pause in the large open space and find a chair to settle into. "I'll wait here until they get in from the party. You can go back if you want to." I glance at each one of them.

Cameron pulls up a seat, Deghan plopping on the couch next to me, and Silas leans against the wall. All of them with no intention to leave anytime soon.

It's only a matter of minutes when the girls come up the stairs. Kyra and Remi eye me instantly and head over, but Lillian turns toward their dorm.

"Willow, you should have seen what happened!" Remi slurs,

her eyeliner smudged and telling a story that she's either been crying or laughing. "Lillian smacked Allie."

"What? Why?" I stand, eager for answers.

Kyra laughs. "I thought I was the scary one. Lills straight-up got in Allie's face and laced her with a good one. Allie was appalled. Oh em gee, it was the best thing I've ever witnessed. Her expression. It was priceless." She busts out laughing, doubling over and falling into Remi.

"Is she okay? Lillian?" I glance toward where she disappeared.

"She'll be fine, that little firecracker." Kyra hiccups, throwing her hand over her mouth. "Oh no."

"Come on, drunk ass." Remi clutches Kyra's arm and looks to me. "Walk us home?"

"Of course."

The guys stay behind, and I take Remi's free hand and lead her to her room.

"You have an entire entourage of hot guys at your disposal, Willow. It's no wonder you've been too busy for us." Remi winks. "I can't say I blame you."

"We're friends," I add.

"Friends? That's funny. Have you seen the way each of them watches you, their eyes glued to you? They may be your friends, but you're not theirs, at least not completely. They *all* have the hots for you."

I shift the attention from me to her. "What about you? Anyone caught your eye?"

Remi glances over at Kyra and says, "You know me, I'm keeping my options open."

We arrive at the door and pile together for a group hug. Being in their company is such a welcome addition.

"Let's get breakfast in the morning," Kyra suggests.

Remi pulls back, her eyes going wide. "Yes, yes, yes!"

"Okay," I give in, despite the uncertainty of what my morning will bring. "Tell Lillian I said goodnight."

The girls funnel into their room and leave me in the corridor alone. I lower my head and mosey down the hall.

"I'm beat." Cameron yawns, stretching his arms. He meets me near the entrance of the dorm lobby. "You going to be okay?" He reels me in for a hug.

"Yep, I'm heading to bed, too. It's been a long day." I squeeze him gently.

He turns to the guys, waving and saying, "Night."

Now, all that remains is Deghan, Silas, and me.

"Okay, now it's my turn." Deghan wraps his arms around me and lifts me off the floor a hair. "Night, tiny one." He releases me all too soon.

"Sleep well." I scan his chestnut eyes.

Once he's gone, Silas says, "Are you going to tell me what's going on?" His voice is strained with concern. "I'm not a fool, Willow. Don't shut me out." He closes the gap between us until he's standing right in front of me. "What is it?" His words are merely a flutter.

"I...I can't." I swallow and shake my head.

He frowns, taking his hand and resting it along my cheek.

I close my eyes in response and lean into his touch.

"What's hurting you?"

"I'm not sure. It's nothing I can make sense of." I open my eyes and find his staring back at mine. Gray and silver with shades of purple weaved in. They're impossibly breathtaking, and each time he looks at me, a shock wave courses through me. Is this how he looks at everyone or is it only me?

*"He doesn't want you."*

"There, right there, that one was the most intense of them all. I *felt* it, Willow."

"Some things are better left unsaid, like talking about fate." Sure, it's a low blow, but if I want him to stop prying, I have to give him a small taste of his own medicine. Part of me is immensely drawn to divulging my deepest darkest fears to him, but the other—rational—side of me, is aware of how exposed that would leave me.

Pain takes over his face as I slam the mental door on him.

*"That's it, push him away. Destroy him before he destroys you. He'll never love you."*

"I'm sorry," I say. "I'm not trying to hurt you. I'm not ready to talk about it yet."

He nods. "Okay. I'll be here when you're ready." Taking my hand in his, he guides me to the west dorm.

We reach my room, and I itch to ask him to stay, but I don't. It wouldn't be fair of me.

I stand on my tiptoes, pressing a soft kiss on his cheek. I sigh, not prepared to deal with a night full of his absence.

I settle into my room, and the silence and loneliness kicks in full force.

*"You're always going to be alone."*

"What do you want from me?" I ask the voice.

*"You're crazy, Willow. Following in line with your mother. Talking to yourself."*

"Says the voice in my head."

Quiet ensues, and I grow certain I've been making up the thoughts. I allow myself to relax, falling into a deep sleep.

Demons haunt me in my dreams, and I'm flooded with the realization that I'm bound to hurt everyone I care about. It wrecks me, robs me of any peace I had within, and leaves me sweating, burning up, screaming, and gasping for air.

*Please, someone, anyone, help me.*

# CHAPTER 7

S haking, rattling, a firm grip.

"Willow, wake up." Silas urges me into the present.

I awake in a panic, shoving him and scooting back on the bed, bringing the covers with me in an attempt to protect myself. I frantically look him over, glance down at my own arms and body. I'm here, I'm not dreaming anymore, but why is the fear so real and still coursing through me?

He holds up his hands. "I'm not going to hurt you. I could hear you screaming. Are you okay?"

*"Coward."*

Tears fall down my cheeks, and I'm not sure how long I've been crying.

Silas scans my body. "Are you hurt? Please tell me what's wrong."

I wipe at my face. "I'm okay. It was a nightmare, that's all."

"A nightmare?" He shakes his head. "I can *feel* your hurt. Whatever you're going through, I'm experiencing it, too."

My eyes are heavy despite me being so damn afraid of the thing haunting me. "Will you stay with me?" My bottom lip quivers.

*"Pathetic and weak."*

"Yeah, absolutely." He stands, grabbing on to the nearby bed. The legs scratch the floor as he brings it over. Silas sits, only a few inches away, on the other bed.

"Can you come closer?" I reposition myself to give him room.

Hesitantly, he positions himself next to me, kicking off his shoes and bringing his legs up. He holds out his arm, inviting me in, and I'm not sure there's anything in the world that sounds sweeter than being this near him.

I relax into the curve of his arm, nestling in comfortably. I place my hand on his chest and grow aware of the absence of a heartbeat. My nerves calm, but there's still a wicked terror lying in wait.

He draws me in tighter, kissing the top of my forehead. It's soft and warm and everything I needed in this moment.

I fall back asleep, but this time, his presence rids the demons from ruining me.

---

I wake and am completely startled by my reality. Somehow, Silas is still here, holding me like he may never let me go.

Not wanting to end this heaven on earth, I continue to lie there, soaking him in.

"You were snoring," he breaks the silence.

I sit up in a hurry. "Was not." I smooth my hair down that's sticking up on the side.

He smiles. "You're somehow even more beautiful in the morning."

"All lies," I tease, jumping from the bed to brush my teeth. It's one thing for him to see my bed head, but I'm not about to subject him to my morning breath.

I come back to find him putting on his shoes. Sadness courses through me at the reality that he's going to leave. I'll never quite get used to the total body deficiency I have without him.

"See you shortly." He touches my face with his hand, running his thumb along my bottom lip in the sexiest way possible. He grins, seeming to know he's driving me wild.

Upon his exit, I wash my face and change out of my clothes, hoping that I haven't missed the girls going to breakfast.

I leave my lonely room and shut the door at the same time another closes. It's the short, dark-haired girl I've avoided since I moved to the supernatural dorms.

"Hey," I offer. "I'm Willow." I extend my hand. "We haven't formally met, and that's totally my fault. I've been a basket case for a while now and have pretty much dodged everyone I could. Oh god, I'm rambling. I'm sorry. Wow, bad first impression."

She smirks. "I know who you are. Headmaster Walker filled me in when you switched dorms. I'm Ruby."

We shake, and cooling energy pulses from her into me.

"Listen, I don't mean to cut this short, but I have to run. We should get coffee soon," she says.

"Yeah, I'd love that."

She departs, and I stagger my own descent, not wanting to follow her closely.

I cross into the open area, stepping along the glass floor that to this day still amazes me. It unravels my stomach to look down, the tree and shrubbery just a shattered surface away. The architecture in this building is out of this world. Who thought to have an indoor, enclosed garden in the middle of a stone building? Not to mention building it well enough so it doesn't collapse in on itself.

Without giving it another thought, I enter the south wing hallway, pausing in front of the girls' door. Rustling sounds fill the space, reassuring me that they're still in here.

I knock.

The door opens a moment later.

Lillian. She stares at me and then turns away, going back into the room. Silent treatment it is.

I poke my head inside. "Morning."

Remi beams, and Kyra scowls.

"My head!" Kyra whines. "I forgot to take Tylenol last night, and now...uh..."

I cross my arms and lean against the threshold. "I don't feel sorry for you."

"You're cruel, Willow."

I laugh. "You brought it upon yourself. Let's get breakfast. I've heard that'll help with hangovers. Or, you could always try the hair of the dog."

"Nuh-uh, no way in hell am I so much as *thinking* about alcohol today." She grabs her clutch off the table next to her bed and mopes toward me, her brown curls bobbing with each step.

"You two go ahead, we'll be down in a minute." Remi closes a makeup compact and picks up her mascara.

I glance at Lillian on the way out. With her back to me, she's laying it on thick, and boy is it working. She continues to break my heart with her distance, but I can't blame her, that wouldn't be fair.

I weave my arm through Kyra's. "Some caffeine should help. Want to stop in the teacher's lounge and get some of the good stuff?"

"Girl, you are speaking my language."

Brooke and I have been friends for a long time, and we've had a great relationship, but this, the thing I have with these three girls, it's entirely new and exciting and fulfilling in a way I never knew I was missing until I had it in my life.

Locked together, we make our way down the stairs and through the main lobby, to the north wing.

The scent of coffee fills the air and distracts me slightly from the weird energy of this side of the school. I guide Kyra to a seat and stand in front of her, raising my chin. "Your order, my lady?"

"You're on one." She snorts. "I'll have a latte, please. Vanilla. Skim."

"Coming right up," I cheer, spinning on my heel. I push a few buttons and obtain the milk.

"Lillian will eventually get over it, don't worry too much."

Her words stop me in my process. I nod. "Yeah, it sucks. She's rightfully justified in feeling the way she does, I just hope it doesn't last forever. I miss her."

"She misses you, too. And I think that's why it was so hard on her. You two became really close super-fast, so for you to straight up dip, it was a lot on her."

"You're right. I was wrong. I should have made more of an effort, and I promise from here on out I will. I've been dealing with some personal shit, and it's been a lot to handle on my own. There wasn't a day that went by that I didn't think about you girls, though."

I pour her espresso in the cup and finish making her coffee. I place it on the desk near her and go back to finish my own, aware that it'll never be as good as Sydney making it. He must use magic, because I've followed his recipe numerous times, and it never quite comes out the same.

A crackle of energy bolts through me, and I do a quick scan of the room, not wanting to draw attention to myself from Kyra. Although the shadow realm is deactivated, I'm still fearful that it'll somehow reopen, and I'll be sucked in to fight another demon, this time falling to my demise, or worse, hurting someone innocent.

Being friends with me is dangerous, especially with my cursed magic and the fact that I've made no progress on figuring out any of the details of the origins of the dreaded curse.

I haven't even determined what this next curse will be.

*"You're a failure, a fool, a stupid girl."*

I suck in a breath, the pain of the words lashing me internally.

*"You can't protect them."*

My focus shifts to Kyra, sitting at her little area, blowing on her steaming cup of coffee, fully oblivious to my erratic behavior.

Maybe I never should have given them their memories back. Maybe they really would have been better off without me in their lives. They would have been safe, happier, too. But isn't letting them have the part of the truth they're capable of receiving better than stealing something that's rightfully theirs? How will I ever know what the right decision was?

"This is straight-up heaven." Kyra holds her mug like it's the most precious thing in the world.

"You can thank Sydney for teaching me." I grab my cup and walk to the door.

"Ohh, is he one of your many admirers?" She follows me over.

I chuckle. "Something like that."

We make our way back out into the lobby, Cameron and a couple of his friends joining us.

"How'd you sleep?" Cam nudges me.

"Meh, you?" The first part of the night was terrible, the terrifying nightmares, but once Silas joined me, I slept soundly, so much that I allegedly snored.

"I never really sleep well if I'm being honest," Cam declares.

I had no idea he had trouble sleeping. I guess we all do now that I think about it. Silas is, well, a vampire, so naturally, he doesn't sleep much. Deghan complained he hadn't been sleeping well, and Sydney lives off coffee because of his own lack of rest.

I'll have to see if I can figure out a way to help all of us sleep. There has to be a spell or a crystal that could do the trick. I should check with Abigail the next chance I get.

We enter the dining hall, filing toward our destination. Food.

I grab a couple of breakfast burritos and a cup of salsa and find a place to sit. It's not long until our table is full, and everyone is chatting up a storm.

The girls. Half of the guys—Cameron and now Deghan. And some of their friends, including Lillian's guy, Ethan.

The two of them sit next to each other, and for a second, I watch them. I try not to be a creep, but I really am so happy that Lillian found someone who brings her joy.

"So," Deghan interrupts. "Who's coming for family day?"

I swallow the bite of food in my mouth. "Family day?"

"Yeah, not this coming week, but the next. They do it every year. Everyone has their parents or whoever come."

"Really?" I take a sip of the tea Cameron brought me.

"Mmhm. They encourage us to give them a tour, eat lunch together, introduce them to our friends and teachers and stuff." Deghan shoves a large piece of pancake in his mouth, syrup oozing out.

I reach out, wiping my thumb across the mess on his lip, licking it off of myself.

"Okay, never do that ever again," he says, wide-eyed.

"Oh god, I'm sorry."

"Don't be. That was the hottest, most unexpected thing I've experienced."

I smack him. "Whatever."

Through another bite, he mumbles, "No joke."

I focus back on my food, not containing my smile. "Who are you bringing?"

"Aunt and uncle, probably. They're kinda busy all the time...I wouldn't be surprised if they don't make it."

I nod. "I should probably call my mom and tell her. Maybe she and my uncle could drive over. We only live ten minutes away."

"No shit? I didn't realize you were from here." He glances across the table to Cam.

"That's what I said," Cameron adds. "Willow's been hiding out from us all these years." He winks at me.

I finish the last few bites of my food and clear my trash. "I'll see you guys later. I'm going to see if I can borrow Walker's landline."

# CHAPTER 8

"Willow, what can I help you with?" Headmaster Walker asks from his seat behind his desk.

"Do you mind if I borrow the phone? I want to ask my mom about the family day thing." I stay in the doorway.

He shuts his laptop and stands, his tall frame high above the desk. He must be at least six feet tall, about the same height as Deghan. "Sure, I was needing to get another coffee anyway. Take your time."

"Thanks." I smile. "I was curious about something, though, if you don't mind me asking."

"What's up?" His expression is welcoming.

"With locking the school down like you have, how does that

impact people coming in and out on family day?" I make sure my voice is low enough to not bring any unwanted attention.

"That is a valid concern. Basically, the leaving isn't the issue, but the incoming traffic is, so I've formed a team to scan everyone visiting the school, especially those with supernatural abilities. No more than two people per supernatural student can visit, which shouldn't be an issue, and only approved visitors."

"Approved visitors?"

"Meaning anyone on your emergency contact form. We don't need any strange second cousin twice removed visiting out of the blue. Moms, dads, siblings, aunts, and uncles...those are all acceptable." He grips his chin in his hand and tilts his head. "Didn't you get the memo?"

"No, I must have missed it with everything going on. My mom and uncle are okay, right?" I better make sure prior to calling and asking her to come.

He nods. "Yep, you're good to go." Walker strides toward the door.

I step inside and out of his way.

He stops just shy of leaving. "I assure you that I will do everything in my power to keep you and everyone at the school safe." And with that, he heads out.

I get comfortable in his chair and pull the phone off the charging dock, punching in the numbers I've memorized by heart.

It rings three times, and a familiar voice shines through. "Hello?"

"Hey, it's me." I make note of how...*happy* she seems.

"Willow, sweetie, hi. Is everything all right?" Mom asks.

"Yes, all good. How are things there?"

"Great, wonderful really. I'm feeling *much* like myself, more so than I have in such a long time. I've even got Danny to get off my back a bit." She laughs.

"I'm so relieved to hear that. Which brings me to why I called."

"Yes, of course. What's going on?"

"There's this family day coming up. I'm only just now finding out about it because of everything that's kept me occupied, but if you don't think Danny is too busy, maybe you two could come? It's on the Wednesday following next." I hold my breath, not sure what the response will be.

"Let me see here..." She rustles with something in the background. "Danny has that day scheduled off of work, so that would be perfect timing."

I exhale. "Really?"

"Yes, honey. We'd love to come visit you. What a wonderful surprise!"

"That's great. I can't wait to see you." My heart swells with emotion.

"Likewise." A buzzer goes off. "Hey, I don't mean to cut you off, but I've got to get my muffins out of the oven."

"Muffins?" I call out. "Don't tell me they're blueberry."

"Guilty," she admits. "I'll bake you a fresh batch for our visit. Deal?"

"You're the best."

"Love you, sweetheart."

"Love you, too, Mom. See you soon."

I hang up, reeling in the relief that she's still doing okay and I'll be seeing her soon. If it were up to me, I would have spent the weekend there, but with the new orders of keeping the school secure, I'm unable. Despite the demon breaking through the shadow realm, the academy really probably is the safest place for me, especially with having the guys around. Not sure I could have made it out of the demon attack without them.

Walker peeks his head into the office. "I'm not trying to rush you. I walked by and saw you hang up."

"I'm finished." I push in the chair and make my way around the desk. "I appreciate it."

"No problem at all. The service here sucks. It's partly the old building, but it's also because of the wards put in to protect the school. It blocks out some of the frequencies of the cell towers. We're constantly updating the internet and keep accidentally breaking it." He laughs. "I did need to speak with you, though." His tone becomes more serious.

I stop my exit out of the office. "Yeah?"

"We could use your help with the realm repair if you're still interested."

Here I was thinking he was about to kick me out of the school for some random reason, and instead he's recruiting me for an incredibly important project.

"Whatever you need. I broke it, I feel obligated to fix it."

"You'll be starting back to your regular classes tomorrow, but if you don't mind me pulling you early from a few of them, we could begin then. I checked your grades, and you're excelling in all of your coursework, so I don't foresee any issues. It's not your responsibility, and you're not obligated to help, even if you don't want to. Don't feel bad if you want to sit this one out."

"No, absolutely. I'd love to help. I'm truly thankful to be here. It's the least I could do."

"Another thing, too, is around this time in the term, the lectures become shorter, allowing more time for completing those pesky papers and projects and studying for exams. Use that time however you see fit. I'm aware you're chomping at the bit to make progress on your curse, so I encourage you to utilize it wisely."

Is he giving me permission to blow off my homework and study magic? I am pretty well caught up, despite the circumstances, with only a few outstanding assignments left to complete. It wouldn't be too difficult to balance focusing more on my personal research.

Abigail walks into the room. "Am I interrupting?"

We shake our heads.

"Not at all," Walker confirms. "Was having a chat with Willow."

She hands him a stack of papers. "Here's the information you requested."

"Ah, perfect. Thanks, Abigail." He takes it, adjusts his glasses, and flips through a few pages. "Willow will be joining us tomorrow," he adds without taking his eyes off the document.

"You have so much going on," she says. "Are you sure?"

"You two keep acting like there's a choice in the matter. I'm helping—end of story."

I spend the rest of the morning in the library, burning my eyes over the pages of this book I can't seem to figure out. I had to use the beacon Abigail gave me. I totally thought I could find the room on my own but I epically failed.

I realize I've been in the library too long when my stomach growls, alerting me that it's probably past lunchtime. I take the bottle of water out of my backpack and drink the rest of the contents, shaking the last few drops into my mouth. Hopefully, it'll buy me a little more time.

*"Failure."*

I push the thought away, scanning the text further. If I'm an Oliver witch, why can't I make sense of the damn Oliver witch book? How is it possible I can be so oblivious?

*"Because you are nothing. And you never will be."*

Furious, I snap the book shut and latch on to another one from the table.

"I will figure this out," I huff.

*"You will never learn. You are a fool, a pitiful embarrassment to the Oliver name."*

"I'm a fool but I broke the first curse?" I respond to the voice in my head.

*"By chance. Your efforts are pointless. You're not capable enough to figure this out. You will ruin the Oliver name. You will strip your mother of her powers. You will lose your father forever. You will put everyone you love in danger. And the saddest thing of all, knowing that none of them ever loved you. Give up, Willow."*

I swallow, shifting my gaze across the room. Is this real? Are these my thoughts? It's my voice but different. Threatening, dark. What is happening?

I sink to the floor, the old musty book still clutched in my hands.

*"Weak. The world would be a better place without you."*

I grasp at my chest. Air constricting. A weight heavy on my shoulders.

*"It hurts you because it's true."*

I dig my nails into the cold, hard floor, desperately trying to ground myself. A sharp pain pierces my hand and, glancing down, I spot my bloody fingers. Everything goes silent except the pounding beat of my heart.

Sweat rolls down my neck, trailing my spine. My other hand shakes, and I hold it in front of my body, trying but unable to keep it from trembling.

Sounds come back the second Silas bursts through the door, screeching to a halt next to me.

"Willow, breathe. You're having a panic attack." He rests his hands on my shoulders.

"I am?" I ask, confusion settling in.

"Close your eyes. Focus on your breathing. Focus on me. Focus on anything that makes you happy."

I open my eyes back up, settling my sights on him, staring intently into his gray eyes. I take in a breath, thinking about Deghan, exhale, Cameron, inhale, Sydney…again, the girls.

My heart slows its pace, the heaviness on my chest easing.

"You have to tell me what's going on. Please let me help you." He brings me onto his lap. "You have me so worried. I'm not lying when I say I can *feel* your hurt, Willow."

"There are voices," I whisper.

He looks me over. "Voices?"

"In my head." I must sound like such a whack job.

"What are they saying?" Silas is kind with his question, treating me as if I'm a fragile child.

"They're cruel." Tears fill my eyes. "They tell me everything I'm afraid of. I...I'm not sure which are my thoughts anymore."

He tugs me into him, and I feel protected in his arms, his black cotton T-shirt cool against my warm face.

*"He'll never love you."*

"What did that one say?" he mutters into my hair.

I shake my head. "I can't."

"Whatever it was, it's not true. Something is playing tricks on your mind. It's telling you lies, please believe that."

I bite my lip, begging the tears to stop coming and for his words to be the truth.

"As much as I hate saying this, we should probably go talk to Sydney. He might be able to help." With the mention of Sydney, his voice deepens.

I wish they didn't hate each other so damn much.

*"They're going to hate you, too. You'll ruin them all."*

"Up. Come on. We're going now. I can't stand for you to be going through this."

I get to my feet with his assistance, setting the book on the table and grabbing my bag.

"How long have you been down here?" His tone is accusatory.

"Since breakfast, why?"

"Willow, it's dinnertime. Have you eaten?"

I shake my head, dizziness hitting me.

He sighs with force. "You're a witch, Willow. You have to make sure you're eating. It sounds silly, but if your energy is depleted by all this information you're trying to learn, and you're not replenishing yourself naturally, you'll crash harder. It's no wonder you're in the state that you are."

I look to the floor, ashamed of being so foolish. "I'm sorry."

"It's nothing to apologize for, although I'm pissed that no one has told you this stuff. It's fundamental for your kind. Food, water, rest." He leads me out of the room, his hand on the small of my back.

I slow my pace and encourage his hand to press more firmly to move me along. His touch calms my aching soul.

Moments later, we appear in the main library, and then up the stairs into the foyer. The trek drags on. Each step I lose a little bit more energy.

"Do you have that pen on you?" Silas asks.

I reach into my pocket and hand it to him. "Why?"

His gaze shifts around and he nudges us toward a large pillar in the sitting room, blocking us from wandering eyes. Grasping my hand, he clicks the pen, and we go invisible.

His hands find their way to my body, and he lifts me off the floor.

Relief floods in to not have to walk anymore. I'll never get used to how freely we can touch now that whatever was blocking us in the past is gone. I had once thought that we never stood a chance, deadly electricity pulsing between us, but now the energy is fierce, only this time in a purely wonderful way.

"How many times are you going to have to carry me to Sydney? This is becoming a bit embarrassing." My head bobs and I wrap my arms around his neck, pulling myself in tight. His woodsy scent is enough to calm my nerves.

"I don't enjoy it one bit. I'd give anything to be the one to rescue you." His words have such a hint of sadness in them.

"You're the one who rescues me. Don't for a second think that's not the case. He heals me; you're the one who saves me, though."

We arrive at Sydney's door, and he sets me to the floor, making us visible again.

I knock. A second later, Sydney opens the door.

At first, his face reads excitement and then disdain when he settles on Silas.

"What can I help you with?" He's clearly irritated.

"If you're busy, we can come back," I say, a little hurt at his reaction.

"Can we come in? There's been a *development*." Silas is firm and authoritative.

Sydney looks from Silas to me, then back again. "Yeah," he finally allows.

Stepping inside, Silas shuts the door behind him. He crosses his arms, waiting for me to speak.

"Someone get to it," Sydney asserts.

"Do you have any snacks?" I sway to one side.

"You came here for something to eat?" He scans me and then decides to grab a granola bar from his desk.

I tear it open, biting into it hastily.

"Willow has voices in her head. Have you heard of anything like this? I'm assuming it's the next curse. It's causing her a great deal of pain, and she had an anxiety attack, *alone*, in our side of the library."

Sydney's eyes go wide. "Angels, Willow. Are you okay? I'm sorry. Here..." He holds out his hands to guide me. "Sit." He directs me onto a spare bed.

"How bad is it?" he asks Silas.

Why would he ask him and not me?

"It's bad...especially if it hurts me."

# CHAPTER 9

Twenty minutes of Sydney running his hands up and down my body go by, and no progress is made.

"I don't understand." He rubs his head. "I can't sense the energy. I should be able to find it, locate its source, and pull it out."

"If it's the curse, it might be deeper rooted than that. Not something you can simply get rid of in traditional ways," Silas suggests.

"You both know I'm *right* here, don't you? You're talking like I'm not in the room." I lean back onto my elbows, my energy already coming back a little from the granola bar I ate.

Sydney drops to his knees beside me, his hand on my knee. "Willow." He looks to my eyes, his face blank of emotion. "I can't fix this."

I reach up, gripping his hand in mine. "I didn't expect you to. You don't always have to be the one to fix me. But now we're aware that this isn't some ordinary thing, right? So, we can start pinpointing the curse's origins. That's good enough." I say the words, but they come out flatter than I expect.

Did I hope Sydney could get rid of what is going on in my head? Hell yeah. But I knew damn well coming here that I couldn't be so lucky, this was my problem to resolve on my own.

"I can help, though, with the research, with some protective spells. There are certain things we can do to up your defenses and make this more...*tolerable*, until we find a permanent solution." He holds my hand firmly and offers a weak and forced smile. "I'm sorry."

"Someone should be near her at all times, for precautionary measures. I can't imagine what would have happened if I didn't find her when I did." Silas radiates fear and concern. His lips pressed in a hard line—he almost looks...soldiery. Ready for battle.

"Bodyguards? Are you serious? Don't overreact. This was the first time this has happened, and it's probably because I didn't eat lunch." I glance to Sydney for some kind of backup.

"You didn't eat? Willow, that's one of the golden rules." His head lowers. "We are failing you here." He sighs. "You have to eat, even something little every so often. You're learning so much and you can't deplete your energy stores without replenishing them. It leaves you vulnerable, weak to attack." He swings his attention to Silas. "I hate to say this, but he might be right...at least until we figure out what's going on."

Silas stiffens. "We'll have to fill everyone in. None of us have class with her anymore, so that poses an issue. We can take—"

He's interrupted by a knock at the door. Sydney walks over and cracks it, then opens it fully, allowing Deghan entry.

"Dude, I was so worried. Where have you guys been?" he says.

"We have a problem," Sydney tells him.

Deghan immediately looks to me, his eyes scanning up and

down. He closes the space between us before anyone can explain. "What's wrong?"

How did I get so lucky to have all of these guys care about me so much? It's like I hit the jackpot.

Silas speaks. "The next curse, it's something in her head. A voice. It caused her to have a panic attack, and I can't imagine what would have happened if I hadn't gotten there. Sydney can't get rid of it, and until we figure out how to do so, she's going to need constant surveillance."

Deghan nods. "Yeah, we can take turns. There are enough of us." He sits on the bed next to me, wrapping his arm around my shoulder and pulling me in, suffocating me with his embrace like he always does.

I smile at how much I love it. It's such a Deghan hug.

---

We make our rounds, and boy is it uncomfortable.

It's something similar to, *Hey, guys, I'm a little defective and need someone around me because I'm incapable of feeding myself properly.*

Luckily, Sydney and Silas do most of the talking. I just answer the questions that are asked.

Cameron is on board, always jumping to be of some help. I'm sure he feels a tiny bit inadequate, not having any supernatural abilities, but I value his presence all the same.

Abigail is busy somewhere, running errands for Walker, so we'll have to find her when she returns and fill her in on the shit situation.

Walker goes into total Dad mode upon learning the latest development.

"Willow, you poor thing. May I take a look?" He turns his hand over in front of me.

I nod.

He scans me with his palms, a moment later stopping and

exhaling loudly. "I hate that this is happening to you. The guys are right, though. I'll get with Abigail and see what I can do about reworking your schedule again. Actually…" He looks away and to nothing, lost in thought. "We're near the end of the term, and you're excelling. I could speak with your professors directly and see about excusing you from class, with the circumstance that you'll complete your assignments under either my or Abigail's supervision. I'm sure Professor Tremont would be of assistance, too." He starts counting on his fingers. "Me, Abigail, Tremont, Silas, Deghan, Sydney…"

"And Cameron," I add.

"And Cameron," he confirms. "That should suffice, wouldn't you say?"

Great, I have seven people who are going to be hovering around me non-stop for the foreseeable future. It's not that I'm ungrateful, but at what point do I get time to do basic human needs, like using the bathroom? At least I won't be alone, though, and somehow, I find comfort in that. Especially considering when I'm surrounded, the voices seem to stay at bay. Maybe this is a good plan after all.

"I'm going to put on the table that if you're not comfortable with the project we discussed, you're more than welcome to decline." Walker seems genuine.

"I'm good. I'd prefer to keep some sort of semblance of normalcy going, if that's okay."

"Understandable." He glances down at a tablet on his desk, poking his finger along the screen. "Meet me in here for first period, and we can discuss with Abigail how to best move forward with your schedule."

Silas, Sydney, Deghan, and I funnel out of Walker's office.

"I can take over from here," Deghan suggests. "You two can go get rested up. You need all of your strength." He motions to Sydney. "And you probably need to *replenish*," he says to Silas.

Silas stiffens in response, his jaw tightening. "I won't be long, okay?" His eyes bore into me.

"You're hungry, too, and I could always eat." Deghan smiles my way.

"Go eat," Sydney interjects. "But stop by my room on your way back through, I'll have a few things for you."

Sydney heads to his room, and Silas holds firm, clearly not wanting to leave.

He reaches out toward me right as Deghan weaves his fingers between mine, dragging me away.

"Come find us when you're done, pretty boy," Deghan teases.

I look over my shoulder, watching Silas until he's out of sight, the void of him opening up inside me.

Walking into the dining hall, I quickly notice how empty it is. I must have really lost track of time and missed lunch and dinner service.

Deghan leads us toward a door in the corner. He knocks twice and smiles at me.

The entry creaks open and, low and behold, Cameron appears. "You're just in time."

"For what?" I ask.

Deghan tugs me inside, following Cameron.

The space is immense, a kitchen bigger than I've ever seen. Metal everything, and clean, white walls. Vast workspaces and commercial-sized sinks and ovens.

Cameron pulls the handle on what I thought was a pantry but turns out to be a massive refrigerator. He takes out a pack of mushrooms and bell peppers, sets them on the counter, and grabs a clove of garlic and a hefty knife. He salts a pot of already boiling water.

"You can cook, too?" I blurt out.

He beams. "A little."

Deghan stands in front of me, his hands wrapping around my waist, hoisting me up and sitting me on the counter. "Don't let him fool you," he says once I'm secured. "I'd starve if it weren't for him making me extra food."

"I had no idea." I knew they were friends, but I didn't realize they were *this* close. It's such a wonderful surprise.

Cameron lays the knife sideways on the garlic, smashing his hand onto it to break it open. He peels away the skin and finely chops the remaining pieces. He tosses them into a sizzling skillet, the rich aroma immediately coursing about. Dropping the pasta in the water, he turns to me and winks.

To see him in his element is so sexy. He radiates such confidence, not that he's ever lacking, which takes my attraction to him to another level.

Cameron slices the veggies, plopping them into separate skillets. The mushrooms go with the sautéed garlic and the peppers on their own.

"Why not together?" I ask.

"I want them to keep their own flavors," he replies without hesitation.

Deghan smirks from beside me. "You thirsty?" He strolls to the fridge and brings out a pitcher of tea. "Cameron brewed you some fresh, unsweet, how you usually have it."

I bite my lip to hide my grin. "Did I die and go to heaven? Is this some alternate universe? Why are you guys being so nice to me?"

Deghan pulls out a glass and responds, "Because we care, and you're going through a lot of shit right now. Why wouldn't we want to make things easier on you if possible?"

A buzzer goes off, and Cam reaches for a mitt, taking a pan of chicken out of the oven. The room fills with more decadent smells.

"Do you need a hand?" I can't help but notice he has a lot of things going at once.

"Nope, I'm good. I promise. Trust me." He stirs the vegetables and checks on the pasta.

"Here ya go." Deghan places my drink next to me.

I take a healthy swig.

"Thank you." I shift from Deghan to Cameron. "Where did

you learn how to cook?" I set the cup back down and focus on him.

His shoulders tense for a second. "Had no other choice." He shrugs. "It was only me and my brother growing up. He's older and was gone a lot, so I kinda figured it out on my own. A lot of YouTube, if we're being honest...and trial and error. Oh, man, I made some atrocities..." He lets out a chuckle. "This one time...I was really little. I thought it was a good idea to put vanilla ice cream on my chicken. Let me tell you, *not* a good combo. Peanut butter on a burger, though, now *that* is where it's at. I make this blueberry sauce that goes perfectly on grilled steak. Sounds weird, but don't knock it till you try it."

His confession is yet another surprise, a layer of him I had no knowledge of. I find myself yearning for more.

"You'll have to make it for us someday."

"I keep telling him he needs to open up his own restaurant," Deghan says. "And believe me, I eat a *lot* of food, so it's safe to say I'm a good judge of whether or not it's worthy. And it definitely is." Deghan crosses his arms and leans into the counter.

Cameron adds some butter and random stuff to the skillet with the mushrooms, creating a creamy sauce. He tosses in the peppers and drains the pasta, folding it into the mixture. Very carefully, he slices into the chicken that had been resting off to the side. He gently but rapidly scoops his knife under the meat to pick it up and lays it on top of the noodly creation.

"Voila!" He beams.

Deghan grabs three plates, setting them for Cameron to serve up his concoction.

I take my first bite, making sure to get a little bit of everything, and immediately recognize for sure that I must be dreaming. "You are a mastermind."

# CHAPTER 10

I help Deghan clear the plates and clean up while Cameron relaxes. It's only fair, considering he worked so hard in the kitchen to cook us the best meal I've had in my entire life.

"Now what?" Cameron asks.

"What do you mean?" I dry the dish that Deghan hands me and put it back in its rightful home.

Cameron leans back, rubbing his belly. "Who takes over next? Is there some kind of Willow schedule or something?"

It's a funny sight, considering he's got abs under his navy-blue T-shirt. Other than Sydney, all of my guys are wickedly in shape. And I don't mean to exclude Sydney. I just haven't been *that* close to be certain of whatever is going on under his clothes. Our relationship is quite different than what I have with the rest. Not that I'm complaining, I enjoy the dynamic I have between all of them.

And to this day, I still have no clue how I managed to snag them all *and* keep them around.

I laugh. "Not really." I glance at Deghan. "At least not that I'm aware of."

He scrubs a fork, rinsing it, and giving it to me to dry. "Not yet, but that's not a terrible idea."

"Sydney mentioned going to his room when we were done to get some stuff. So let's do that," I suggest.

"Groucho extreme is probably going to want to take overnight duty." Deghan smirks and holds out another utensil.

"Wow, I bet he loves that one." I lay the knife in its cubby. "He's not all that bad, you know."

"Maybe to you," Cameron adds. "Don't get me wrong, It's not that I hate the guy. He's so...*serious*."

I shrug and toss the now wet towel into the bin with the others.

---

We arrive at Sydney's room to find him packing a small bag.

"Here." He finishes stuffing it full. "I want you to place these around your room. Amethyst, smokey quartz, black obsidian, fire agate...there's a bunch of other ones, too. They're mostly good for protection but they all have different properties, including ridding negative energy or thoughts, boosting energy and happiness... pretty much anything I could think of to help with what you're going through." He holds out a black crystal. "Put this one in your pocket and carry it on you at all times."

I look it over, its jet-black rough exterior imperfectly beautiful. Lines are naturally carved out along it.

"Black tourmaline—one of the most powerful protective stones." He secures a small satchel, placing it in my hand, too. "And this is full of various herbs. Lavender, basil, sage, caraway... to name a few."

"Wow, this is incredible, Sydney." My hands are full of various items. "Thank you."

"It's not much, but it's better than nothing. We still need to work on how to properly utilize this kind of stuff, but this is a start."

His hair is disheveled, and it's obvious from his droopy eyes that he's worn out. It pulls at my heart to see him this way, and I ache to be the one to help him with *his* problems.

"Let me carry that," Cameron says, taking the bag from me and freeing my hands.

I slide the stone into my pocket as I was instructed and reach out to hug Sydney.

He's hesitant at first but then wraps his arms around me. He's not really a hugging type of guy, but I do it anyway.

It's a quick one, but it gives me enough time to say, "I really do appreciate everything you do for me." I grasp him at an arm's length. "More than you'll ever comprehend."

He grins. "Don't forget it. I might be the one needing your help one day."

"Deal."

Deghan, Cameron, and I leave Sydney's, making our way to my dorm in the west wing. When we enter the hall, Silas is standing near my door waiting for us. He stiffens at first glance.

"Did I call it or what?" Deghan boasts.

The three of them help me place the stones around my room and then say their goodbyes.

Deghan hugs me first, tight as always, and waits for Cameron before leaving.

Cam gives me a sweet embrace and tells me, "I'm here if you need me. Anytime. Don't hesitate."

"Thanks, Cam." I savor the moment while it lasts.

Once they're gone, Silas clears his throat. "I'll be right outside if you need me."

"You're not going to stay?"

"I am, but out here." His energy is cold and shut off. He steps outside and closes the door.

I let out a breath. "Okay, then," I say to myself, unsure what the hell crawled up his ass.

Taking the opportunity of being alone, I go to my en suite and turn on the shower, stripping down while it warms. Steam fills the space and covers me like a warm blanket. I hop inside, letting the water cascade down.

*"Fool."* The voice returns. *"You may escape me, but you'll never escape yourself."*

I fight back the panic that courses through me, washing my hair in a rush. I grab my razor, doing an equally quick, and not so great job of shaving my legs. I wince, the blade nicking my thigh and blood pooling out.

"Shit," I exclaim.

A door opens, and a knock rattles the bathroom entrance. "Are you okay?"

"Yeah, I'll be right out." I wipe away the blood and go back to finishing my shower, only to look again and see more trickling down.

I complete my tasks, stepping carefully out of the shower and wrapping myself in a towel. I check under the sink for a first-aid kit or a pack of bandages but come up empty.

"Umm, Silas." How am I supposed to handle this situation, given he's a vampire who feeds on blood, and I'm over here gushing from a shaving accident?

"What's wrong?" His nervous energy pierces the door.

I open it slightly, not sure what to expect.

Automatically, his gaze shifts in the direction of my thigh. "You're injured." His voice is strained.

"Uh, yeah. Is this a problem for you? I kinda need something to cover it, but there isn't anything in here. I'm sorry."

Silas's eyes go soft. "May I?"

His question catches me off guard, and I continue to find

myself unable to read the situation but yet somehow totally trustworthy of him.

I swallow, nodding in the process.

His hand grips the doorframe, pulling the door open. He steps forward, his face betraying nothing.

I take a hesitant stride back, bumping against the vanity.

His eyes lock on to mine, his hands finding their way to my sides, lifting me onto the sink.

I go along with his every move, fully entranced, and loving the uncertainty of every moment.

Silas trails his finger along the sensitive skin around my wound, midway up my thigh.

And it's everything I can do to stop myself from squirming.

He takes the same finger, putting it to his lips and biting through the flesh, causing himself to bleed, too.

I don't take my eyes away for one second.

With the blood on his finger, he runs his finger on top of my wound, the magic throbbing between us, somehow sealing my cut completely shut.

I gasp. "How did you do that?"

Still carefully tending my leg, he replies, "It's part of that fate thing I keep avoiding."

I tilt his head up and force him to look me in the eyes. Without allowing him to retreat, I tug his face toward mine, lingering only a second and then passionately pressing my lips onto his. I kiss him like I'm dying for him to understand.

To understand what he means to me, what he does to me, that I'm hopelessly numb without him.

He grants me access, letting our tongues speak a language only they're capable of. His hands glide over my arms, up to my neck, clasping my face. His response matches mine with a sheer intensity only we are capable of. His hip slides between my knees, spreading my legs.

I wrap them around him, my hands frantically drawing him into me, farther, farther, farther, until he's securing one hand around my body and lifting me off the counter and out of the bathroom, our lips never pausing.

We come to a stop, and not once do I open my eyes to see what's going on.

He lays me onto my bed, my body still wrapped around his, my mouth hungry for more.

Silas pauses, seemingly out of breath, his face only an inch from mine. "If I had a heartbeat, it would be pounding out of my chest right now."

"Shh." I reel him back in.

This time his kisses are slow and steady, as though they're thought-out and more in control, with an aching purpose. He tugs at my lip with his teeth, sending spikes of chills through my body.

It's like nothing I've ever known.

His lips trail my mouth, pausing and kissing the corner, my cheek, that spot right below the ear. He takes his time, leaving his breathy presence wherever he pleases. He caresses my collarbone with his tongue and runs his hands down my arms, latching on to my hands. Straddling my body, he intertwines our fingers, raising my hands above my head, diving back in to push his lips against mine.

I'm so hungry for more, I nearly bump our heads together the second he comes closer. Hands still restrained, I forcibly kiss him, pushing one leg into his to let them free.

He cooperates, and I shove my body into him, my barely hanging on towel and his clothes the only things separating us. If my hands weren't pinned, I'd strip him of his shirt, but despite my wiggling, he doesn't let them free. He's in control, and I'm along for one hell of a ride.

I'm not even mad about it.

A few more minutes of a fiery make-out session pass, and he pauses, his nose resting next to mine.

"You have no idea what you do to me," he says, his breath catching.

I smirk. "It's safe to say I have an idea."

He shakes his head. "I've never felt anything remotely close to this in my entire life."

"Attraction?"

"This isn't *just* attraction, Willow," he declares "It's something I can't explain. It's out of this world." He runs his bottom lip over mine, his eyes closing in response, breathing me in. "It's... the most potent drug known to man, the most intense and powerful force on the planet, it's like all the stars aligned and *finally* something truly amazing came from it. It's beautiful and painful and nothing and everything all at the same time, and I cannot...I will never be able to get enough." His voice cracks, and he removes his hands from mine. He pulls away completely, sitting between my legs. He glances down and then repositions my towel to where it's not almost exposing my lady bits.

A chill covers my body from where his once was. Sensing him shutting down, I beg, "Please don't go."

He looks down at his hands that are resting in his lap. "I don't deserve this..." He shakes his head.

"Silas," I whisper, sitting up and onto my knees next to him. I place my hands on his shoulders, resting my head on his back. I breathe him in deeply. "Who's to say that I do either?"

His head falls into his hands. "I'm not good enough for you, I never will be."

Never could I have imagined that I'd witness such a strong and powerful man be so broken, so conflicted and hurting inside...never could I have imagined the insane calling to piece him back together. We're two souls that were once one, fractured with the only chance of survival being each other.

I tug him to face me, running my knuckles along his cheek.

"Let me be the judge of that."

# CHAPTER 11

At some point in the middle of the night, Silas leaves, because when I open my eyes from a deep sleep, Deghan is sitting on the bed next to mine, a sketchpad resting on his lap, his hand furiously drawing away.

He grins. "Morning, sleepy head."

"Please tell me you're not drawing me." I pull the covers over my head.

"Don't worry, I have a photographic memory."

"This is an invasion of privacy or something," I grumble.

I catch the sound of his rustling, and a second later, a large weight settles over my body.

"You're smashing me," I laugh.

"Come onnnn. I'm hungry. Let's go get breakfast." He pokes me in the sides through the blanket.

I bust out giggling. "Stop or I'm going to pee the bed." I yank back the covering so I can breathe.

He tickles me more, and somehow we end up wrestling, the world coming to an abrupt stop when I end up on top of him.

He reaches his hand forward, gently running it along my cheek, his face serious. "You are something else."

I smile, leaning into his palm. "I thought you were starving?"

His eyebrow raises. "You could say that."

I roll off him and head straight to the bathroom to get ready. I poke my head out of the door. "Hey, toss me those pants." I point to the pair at the foot of my bed.

"You're such a slob," he teases. "Oh, wait, are you bottomless over there?" His eyes go wide, and he exaggerates like he's going to lean over and look but throws them to me instead.

A moment later, I come out, hair braided low and to the side. I'm not really sure what to expect from repairing the shadow realm, but having my hair out of the way is probably preferred. I honestly hope I can help, though, and not get in the way and mess things up more.

What could be worse than destroying the shadow realm? Demolishing the school would suck pretty bad. Here's to hoping I can figure out how to use my magic effectively and less destructively.

Deghan takes my hand in his. "Food first, then I'm taking you to the headmaster's office."

We exit my room, hand in hand, at the same time Ruby is entering hers. Her eyes meet mine, and she closes the door.

"She probably thinks I'm such a weirdo." I sigh.

"What? No. Rubes? She's cool."

"You've met?" I say, trying to meet his stride. His long legs take much bigger steps than my short ones.

"Same pack, yeah."

So, she's a werewolf. I wondered but I didn't want to be intrusive and ask. It seems to be a weird thing to blurt out to someone you don't really know. She more than likely is aware that I'm a witch, especially if Walker had to let the supernatural students in on the whole 'no more supe classes because Willow allowed a demon to join us.'

The craziest thing of all is, I don't *feel* like a witch. I mean, part of me is aware of my power, but the sheer fact that I truly have no idea how to properly use it makes me feel pretty damn inadequate—useless, too. Why isn't there a Witch 101 class I can take to figure out the ins and outs? Abigail is doing her best to teach me, but I still can't help but think I'm a slow learner and not doing as well as I should be.

"Whatcha thinking about?" Deghan eyes me through his thick, lush lashes.

We hop down the last two stairs and turn toward the dining hall.

"Nothin'." I lie.

"Aw, how cute, Willow thinks she can lie to me." He tilts his head and smirks, then switches to serious Deghan. "You don't have to tell me, but please recognize that I'm here for you if you ever need to talk." He releases my hand, latching onto my shoulders. "You hearing that voice right now?"

I shake my head. "No, surprisingly not."

He halts in front of me, grabbing my face between his hands. He gets super close to my forehead and says, "Wherever you are, whoever you are, you better leave her alone. Come pick on someone your own size."

"You have no idea what size they are," I point out.

"Hush," he says. "I mean business."

"Okay, okay. You're delirious, let's get you some food." I take him by the hand and pull him into the cafeteria.

"Mmm...I smell waffles." His eyes light up, and it's straight up the most wholesome thing ever.

We load our trays, mine with much less than his, and head toward an awaiting group.

Cameron welcomes us in immediately, and Remi yells, "Heyyy!"

Lillian looks up from her scrambled eggs but doesn't say a word, shifting her focus back down and then on Ethan beside her.

Cameron leans in. "You should really talk to her," he says in my ear.

I bite into a piece of bacon, and it melts in my mouth. "She hates me."

"No, she doesn't. Her feelings are hurt. Talk to her. I'm serious." He takes a drink of his chocolate milk.

I glance back over to her, my heart aching at missing my friend. Maybe now that my schedule has changed, I can steal the landline phone again to give Brooke a call. I can't exactly tell her the truth about things either, but maybe she can give me some advice on how to approach Lillian.

Wait, or can I? The oath said something about not telling the human *students,* but it didn't actually say anything about outsiders. I'll have to verify that. Not that telling my longest best friend that I'm a witch doesn't sound crazy as hell, but being able to talk to her about it might help settle my nerves about everything. Plus, the shocking news about my dad. Brooke will be elated to hear I might possibly have the chance to meet him.

I should have remembered to ask my mom the other day for his name and see if she could bring something that belonged to him to help me with a tracking spell. Abigail's powers typically only work on people she's already familiar with, so blindly being able to find my dad is off the table. I need information, personal items, some DNA would be useful, too.

In any other scenario, I would drop everything I was doing to immediately go and find him. But considering I have this whole reoccurring curse thing going on and am risking my life and other people's lives at every turn, I have to put my personal problems on the back burner. The first chance I get, though, when I can do so safely, I will do everything in my power to locate him and at least try to see if he wants to be in my life—and in my mom's life.

The way she spoke, it sounded like they had something really special, so I can only imagine he would want to be a part of that, despite how many years have passed. Or maybe he's moved on. Maybe he found someone new, started another family. Or maybe something terrible happened and he's gone. I won't know until I find out, but for now, I have to put it on hold.

That only drives me to be more determined in figuring out what the hell is cursing the Oliver witches. It's mind-blowing that there are no records of it—that no one seems to be able to tell me *who* did it or *how* it happened. If the Oliver witches were so powerful and superior to whoever cursed them, how did they allow it to happen?

I guess those are just some of the questions that will continue to plague me.

"Eat up," Deghan orders. "You'll need your energy for whatever Walker has planned for you today."

I finish my eggs, shove the last piece of bacon in my mouth, and wash it down with what's left of my tea. Somehow, despite having nearly three times the amount of food that I did, Deghan's plate is clean.

He stacks his tray on top of mine and takes them up where the rest of the dirty ones go.

"My lady," he beams, holding out his hand. "Away we go."

I shake my head and smile, nudging Cam and saying, "See you later," to everyone.

Deghan deposits me with Headmaster Walker, verifying that Walker will be "taking over" and that he won't leave me unattended.

"Yes, Deghan." Walker huffs. "I assure you I will keep an eye on Miss Oliver. Sydney will be joining us shortly, too."

"Okay, reach out if you need me." Deghan gives me an awkwardly fast hug like he's wanting to avoid the public display of affection in front of an authority figure.

"Willow, we're going to start today in the north wing." Walker stands, coming around his desk and leaning along the edge. "We have to tackle this from the biggest point of entry, so we're going to be near where the *incident* happened. Again, if you want to back out, I can make other arrangements."

"I'm fine," I say for what seems to be the millionth time. I appreciate his consideration but if I'm capable of destroying the realm, I should be more than willing to help fix it.

"You and Sydney are incredibly powerful, and your magic balances each other out. You're the only two students who we'll be using for this, and I want to make sure you're aware that at any time you aren't comfortable, we can stop. The magic you two have is rare, and it will provide us great resources to do the rebuild, but it will be taxing. I want to be transparent with you throughout the whole thing."

A tiny part of me thinks that we're being used, but the more realistic part confirms that we are, but not maliciously or unjustly. If we weren't students and I was merely friends with the staff here, I would still want to help, especially if I was more capable than someone else.

Sydney walks into the room, his eyes a little brighter than yesterday, like he's actually gotten some rest for a change, the stubble on his face contrasting and bringing out the green of his eyes. "Are we ready?" He hands me a steaming cup of coffee.

"Thanks," I mouth.

"Yes," Walker confirms.

One by one, we head to the place it all happened only a matter of days ago.

The moment I feared for my life, I feared for Cameron and Deghan and Sydney and Silas.

I had thought I'd killed Silas. The pain shattering through me so fierce that I screamed and shattered another freaking realm. Apparently, I disintegrated a demon—something of which I've been told is a perilous feat. Everyone keeps reiterating how strong and potent my magic is...in reality, I had a temper tantrum that I lost control of. Maybe if I were able to use the power on my own free will, then I would believe I was the great witch people make me out to be.

Sydney slows his pace to walk beside me. "You good?"

I nod. "Yeah, did you get some sleep?"

"A little. You?"

"Mmhm." I sip my drink, the warm vanilla foam tickling my lip.

We step inside the room, Abigail already sitting on a desk, jotting something down on a pad of paper.

"Shut that door if you don't mind." She motions.

Sydney closes the door and comes back to stand next to me, his presence a comfort.

Somehow, the voices have been kept at bay, and I'm not sure whether I should be worried or relieved about that.

She glances from each of us to the next. "Let's get started."

I take a breath and prepare for instruction.

"All we need you to do is sit here and hold Sydney's hands. It sounds a bit silly, but you both have a large power source, and combined, it will allow us to use that to do the work we need to do. Imagine...we have to paint a wall, but the only way to get the paint is from you and Sydney. You two sit here and make the paint, and Walker and I will use it." She lowers her head and shakes it. "Wow, that is probably the worst example I've ever given in my life."

"I think I get it. Sit here, hold hands. Got it."

She pulls out two pairs of earmuffs. "But while wearing these."

I laugh. "You're joking."

"No, I need to make sure that you're both completely focused on each other, so canceling out any noise is critical to keeping the flow steady." She hands me one and the other to Sydney. "And last but not least, I need you to try to maintain eye contact."

"Well, I guess it can't really get any weirder. Do you want us to get naked, too?" I tease.

Abigail giggles loudly, and her reddish-orange hair bounces with her. "That might be crossing the line."

Sydney leans in and mutters, "You sure you're okay with this?"

I sit on the seat Abigail guides me to and watch him follow suit, only across from me. Our knees alternate between each other, and I'm thankful I put some pants on, otherwise, we'd be doing a lot of skin to skin.

"Here." Abigail scoots a desk to us, giving us a place to rest our arms.

We put the silencers onto our heads and lock eyes.

Sydney puts his hands on the table reluctantly.

I nod and do the same, sliding my hands under his. At first touch, the magic is sharp and electric, a green aura forming around him. My gaze lingers on my hands, up to my arms—the pinkish-purple glitters on my skin. Watching it come to life is truly incredible.

The two swirl together, and without really understanding how, I recognize both coursing through me.

I remember the task at hand and focus my eyes back on Sydney's. His stare is intense and intimate all in one.

"*Wow,*" I think, only this time it really is my voice and not the *other* me, the evil one.

"*Yeah,*" Sydney says, only not out of his mouth but inside my head.

"*You can hear me?*" I telepathically ask him.

His mouth turns upward. "*I guess so.*"

"*This is insane, how are we doing this?*"

"*Must be magic.*" He winks.

"*Oh my gosh, are you flirting with me?*" I beam.

His cheeks flush. *"Is it working?"*

*"Maybe, you'll have to keep trying and find out."* I attempt to wink back.

*"Wow, that might have been the cutest and most pathetic…"*

*"Hey! You're not getting any points by making fun of me."*

*"You're right."* He calms his expression. *"You doing okay?"*

*"Well, I found out I was a witch not too long ago, that my family is cursed, that demons and werewolves and vampires exist, that my dad might be a living breathing thing, and that I have an alter ego who is trying to tear me apart from the inside. I'd say it's a regular old Monday."* I pause. *"Plus, the normal teenager stuff. Starting at a new school, making friends, pissing them off, all that fun stuff."*

*"For what it's worth, I'm sorry. I can't help but take a little responsibility. I was the one who outed you and all."* His smile is completely erased.

I shake my head slightly, still staring into his glorious eyes. *"No, I don't blame you for one second. You shined the light on my true self and the reality of the world. If anything, I haven't thanked you enough. Especially all the times you've saved my ass. It's simply going to take some figuring out on my behalf."*

*"It's still so hard to believe you had no idea."*

*"You're telling me. What about you though, did you always know?"*

He licks his bottom lip even though when he speaks, it's not aloud. *"For the most part, yeah. I grew up with parents who practiced, so it was always common knowledge, and then when I came into mine, I pretty much knew what to expect. There's obviously so much you have to experience on your own, but I always knew what I would become."*

The magic between us pulses, picks up its pace. It's a strange and wonderful sensation.

*"What are they like? Your parents?"*

*"Really strict. They were pretty hard on me growing up. Very formal and stern with their ideas and ways. We don't often see eye*

*to eye. It's rare that we ever have. But they're family, and you'll learn that family is important to our kind."*

*"How was it growing up?"*

*"If I'm being honest, it was pretty lonely. I spent most of my time face down in books, studying to be better. I always thought that if I read enough, I'd be more powerful than them one day. I didn't have many friends. My parents made sure of that. They don't believe in mixing of the species."*

*"That's terrible. You didn't have any witch friends?"*

He shakes his head. *"Very few covens are worthy enough in my parents' eyes, so no."*

*"That explains why you hate Silas so much."*

I catch a glance of Abigail waving her arms in my peripheral but do my best to keep my focus ahead, on Sydney.

*"Vampires are...how do I say this nicely...they're a contradiction of nature's ideologies. And witches are keen on maintaining the balance in nature. Vampires go against that."*

*"What about werewolves?"*

*"Well, werewolves aren't immortal, and they don't take quite the number of lives that vampires do."*

*"Oh."*

*"I'm not trying to persuade you into not liking him. I get it. And it would be a fruitless cause, especially given his circumstance. It's difficult for me is all."*

*"What do you mean his circumstance?"*

Cooling energy flushes through me, followed by a warming embrace.

*"That's his story to tell. Let me just say, though, he's in deep."*

# CHAPTER 13

Over the next few days, we all find our routines.

Silas spends the nights lurking in the shadows of my bedroom, not daring to bridge the gap and come close again. It pains me that he's holding back, that he's so resistant to letting me in. My soul aches for his in an unexplainable kind of way.

Each morning, I wake to Deghan, and he's all tickles and joy. Deep down, I can sense he's as broken as the rest of us but does a better job of hiding it.

Cameron is a master at being a beautiful disaster, too. He is there at every meal, sure to check on me and confirm that everything is going okay. He pops up in the evening, bringing me snacks and keeping my energy flowing. He's selfless and kind and such a pure soul, despite the sadness that lingers within him.

Sydney and I spend most of our days together, our gazes and hands on each other, telepathically conversing about all the things. Sometimes it's serious, like curses and magic, but other times it's about food and music and normal people stuff.

In the afternoons, I often get breaks to work on non-realm-related things. I take that time to study for the final exams that are coming up, or scouring the texts in the library for any hint of what's happening to me.

The voice comes and goes, telling me horrible things that I fear. There's a part of me that realizes it's the curse, but with each threatening word, a small piece of me shatters into an unbreakable form. A thick and heavy cloak of sadness is steadily built, and despite the efforts of everyone around me, I find it more and more difficult to carry.

I do the thing I'm well aware I shouldn't do: tell no one.

I put on a smile and go about my life. Helping repair the shadow realm, even though it's causing more damage by the day. Continuing my studies and research. Spending time with my guards and making an effort to chat with the girls when I can.

Each passing day, I find myself slipping further away, and I'm in too deep to do a damn thing about it.

Currently, Sydney sits across from me, down in the dungeon of the supernatural part of the library.

Our time together has formed this strange, invisible bond. I grow close to him and revel in the comfort of his presence.

His flirting has only increased, the ability to say things privately giving him a type of confidence he doesn't have in the space outside our minds.

It's not obnoxious or outlandish, though. His remarks are cute and witty, and I think sometimes they surprise both of us.

He glances up from his text. "You'd get more work done if you stopped staring at me."

I don't say anything, but instead, continue to gawk, a grin forming.

Sydney leans back and crosses his arms over his chest. "What is it?"

I shake my head. "Nothing, get back to work."

"It's safe to say I know you well enough by now that *that* look is most definitely not *nothing*."

I bite my lip to hide my smile, my stupid eyes betraying me.

He stands, coming around the table, leaning down and putting his hands on the armrest of my chair. "Tell me." He stares dead into my eyes, the same way we've spent so much time doing this week. He takes my hands into his, and the magic between us courses immediately.

I don't protest. I can only imagine it's similar to a form of ecstasy when they mix.

He kneels in front of me. *"Tell me."* His words appear in my head.

I fight back my rampant thoughts. I can't figure them out myself, let alone tell him. My mind becomes a mess of a million things all at once.

He blushes, perhaps solving the puzzle himself. Letting go of one hand, but still holding onto the other, he tucks a stray strand of silver hair behind my ear. "I like you, too." His emerald eyes melt into mine with such passion and intensity but still maintain a calm and thoughtful demeanor.

"You do?" The words bubble out of my mouth.

He looks down to my lips, and I swallow the nervous energy down.

Leaning forward, he gently cups my face in his hands, pausing to ask a silent permission.

I give him exactly that, closing my eyes and bridging the gap, our noses grazing and our lips touching that much more delicately. It's sweet and soft and fucking perfect.

He maintains such control, stopping after one completely flawless kiss.

My heart stutters out of my chest, desperate for more.

His eyes don't break from mine for a second. "Back to work."

Sydney kisses my nose and stands, walking back to his side of the table.

I sit there, in awe of how that went down. At the beginning of the school year, I thought Sydney hated my guts, and here we are, exchanging decadent kisses and staring into each other's eyes all day.

Oh, how the tables have turned.

A few minutes pass, and I shut my book in defeat. "How in the hell are you getting anything done right now?" I should damn well be focused on the task at hand, but it's incredibly difficult given the circumstances.

He focuses on me with a smile. "I'm more productive with you around. And I've told myself if I can find the thing I'm looking for, I might reward myself."

"Reward?" I stare at him with narrowed eyes.

"Mmhmm." He shifts back down to the book in his hand, running his finger along with the text. Triumphantly, he pokes the page. "Ah-ha. Here we are. I freaking knew it."

"Knew what?" I stand and try to take a peek at his discovery.

He smiles, something he doesn't do all that often. It's bright and warm and radiant. Sydney sets the text down, careful not to close the page, and trails his hand on the table, making his way to me. He continues to glide his fingers up my arm, sending figurative sparks flying.

I meet his gaze, and this time, maintaining his control but with more urgency, he thrusts his lips onto mine, slow and steady.

He barrels into me, and we stagger backward. I put my hands down to steady myself, our mouths dancing in unison. One of his hands wraps around my face, the other slides down my back.

A loud alarm sounds, completely disrupting the moment. Sydney slowly moves back, resting his forehead on mine, taking in a hefty breath.

"Saved by the bell," he whispers and then kisses me once more.

I'm left there practically panting while he reaches across the table for his phone.

He holds it out. "Service is shit, but at least the timer works."

"Yeah…"

"Come on." He nudges my shoulder and goes about stacking his books. "Dinner."

*"You'll never make any progress anyway."* The voice returns.

"Can't we stay a little longer? I promise to stay focused." I have to prove the voice wrong—I will rid myself and the Oliver witches of this curse.

"Nope, absolutely not. You have to eat. That's an order."

"I'm not even hungry," I whine.

"Keep this up and I'm going to have to force-feed you."

It's a joke, but I can sense his seriousness.

"Fine, but can we come back down when we finish? I have to figure *something* out."

His expression softens. "Sure, but not long, you need your sleep, too."

"Such a hypocrite," I tease. "You live off coffee and no sleep."

"That's different," he says. "You're more important."

I laugh. "You're so full of it."

Dinner goes by pretty much the same as any other day, Deghan and Cameron cracking jokes, Sydney lost in thought, the girls chatting with random boys and making plans for the weekend.

"You owe us a date night, Willow," Remi says. "Once a week, remember?"

"What did you have in mind?" I take a bite of my burger.

"Party, duh."

My gaze shifts to the guys. Last time we went to a party, Allie dumped my glitch all over me and nearly ruined my life. Being around alcohol in any capacity isn't a good idea.

She's avoided me like the plague ever since. Lillian's smack to the face must have taught her a lesson to back off.

"We should have a movie night instead," Deghan suggests. "There's a projector upstairs."

I secretly mouth, "Thank you," to him for saving the day. I was panicking not knowing what to say, not wanting to bail on them and mess our relationship up more, but not wanting to put myself in danger.

Remi and Kyra exchange a look.

"Great idea," Remi finally says. "But we get to choose."

Deghan chuckles. "Good enough for me. I'll be the one in the back eating all the popcorn."

"Why am I not surprised?" I add.

We finish our food, and once the girls have left, the guys hang back to figure out what the rest of the night entails.

"I need to study some more, only a half-hour," I plead with them. It sucks how badly I'm inconveniencing their lives, but I feel so close to latching onto something and want to give it one last push for the day.

"I can accompany her," Deghan suggests. "I planned on taking over anyway."

Sydney and I meet each other's gazes, a flush hitting both of our cheeks.

"Unless you had something else planned..." Deghan looks from Sydney to me.

"No," we say in unison.

Cameron laughs out loud. "You two are being super weird." He points to us.

"No, that's fine. I have some work to catch up on in my room. Let me know if you need anything." Sydney nods to Deghan and spares me a glance. "I'll see you in the morning."

"Come find me when you're done in the library. I need help with my math homework," Cameron says.

"You're just looking for an excuse to hang out." Deghan smacks Cam's arm.

Cam flinches and rubs the spot dramatically. "Maybe." He smiles.

Deghan claims my hand in typical Deghan fashion, nearly dragging me away from Cam, looking back over his shoulder to say, "See you in a little while."

We descend into the library, and I get the beacon out to help locate the room.

"You still haven't gotten the hang of this place yet?" Deghan asks.

"Have you? It's endless." I watch the meter move and point us in the right direction.

We enter the room, and the energy still pulses of Sydney. I'm blasted with the memory of only an hour ago. I raise my hand to my lips, resting my fingertips against them. Without wanting to give anything away, I quickly lower it to my side.

I take the book on the top of my stack, opening it back up to where I left off. I scan the page until I find the thing I instinctively knew I would.

Sydney enters the library room. "I forgot my bag," he says, pointing to the one near his seat.

"Hey, have you heard anything about the Laveau family?" I ask him while he's here.

His face tenses. "Not much, why?"

"Their name, it's in here with the Oliver name." I scan him for his reaction.

He shrugs. "They're a coven from New Orleans. If I'm not mistaken, they have ties with the Gardners."

"I've seen that name, too. Maybe if I can contact them, they can help me figure out my past."

Sydney's expression hardens, and he lurches forward. "No, Willow. You have to be careful with who you trust right now."

"I agree with Syd," Deghan adds. "Who's to say they aren't the ones who put the curse on your family?"

"Are they powerful?" My mouth goes dry, anticipation consuming me.

"Very."

# CHAPTER 14

$S$ydney goes the rest of the week in an attempt to ignore me, at least that's what I'm left to believe, considering he is everywhere I'm not.

He has his excuses, though.

Friday, Walker and Abigail scheduled us off from the shadow realm, saying we should take the long weekend to rest up and replenish our energy.

The rest of that day I bounced between being watched by Cameron, Deghan, and then in the evening, Silas.

The girls have scheduled a Saturday evening movie night, and I can't help but guess that Sydney will be nowhere to be found.

*Whatever.*

Maybe he realized that our moment together meant nothing to him, and he regrets finally making a move. Or maybe he has information on the Laveau or Gardner family he's not telling me. His behavior is oddly suspicious, and regardless of his reasoning, I'm in disbelief he'd up and vanish in the way he has.

Especially considering all we've been through. I thought what we had was more than that.

"So," Remi says. "What's with the constant puppy dog thing?"

"What do you mean?" I shift my attention to her.

She points to the door of her dorm and sits next to me on my old bed. "They watch you like a hawk. One of them is always around. It's super extreme. How do you get any privacy?"

I laugh, twirling a rogue piece of string around my finger. "It's not as bad as you think."

"Explain it to me." She pulls her legs up and leans onto one arm. "No judgment."

I shrug. "They're all intense in their own ways. And we've all been through a lot together. It probably doesn't seem that way from the outside, but we really have. I can't imagine my life without any of them."

"That makes sense...What do you like about them?" She studies me in anticipation.

"Well, where do I start?" I gaze at the door. "Deghan is...he's so funny and warm. He doesn't have a bad bone in his body. His smile lights up a room, and he's not afraid to be himself. I don't think I could ever spend enough time with him. He and Cameron are best buds." I chuckle. "Cam is funny, too. And he's probably the nicest person I've ever met. He has such a kind heart and is probably the best listener ever. Sydney is...he's Sydney." I sigh. "He and Silas have a lot in common, despite sort of hating each other. They're both kind of loners and incredibly smart. Sydney is Mr. Fix Everything, and it's really nice to have someone I can rely on like that." Even though he's disappeared on me. "And Silas... he's *intense*. We have this unexplainable bond, this pull to one another. He's greatly misunderstood, to say the least."

"And they're all drop-dead gorgeous," she adds.

I laugh. "Yeah, and that."

"And they're totally okay with fawning over you at the same time? No jealousy?"

I shake my head. "At first, I wasn't sure what to expect, but it sort of happened this way, and now it's like none of us really know anything else. It wasn't really planned."

"Have you hooked up with any of them?"

I hesitate, biting my lip in response.

"Oh my god, or *all* of them?"

I grab the spare pillow and throw it at her, and she screams.

At that, the door comes flying open, and Deghan nearly falls to the floor. He quickly rebounds, his cheeks flushing from what I assume is embarrassment.

"Did you fall asleep standing up again?" I ask.

Remi busts out laughing. "Wait, that's a thing that happens often?"

He rubs his neck. "Uhh." He goes to shut the door, but I stop him.

"Hold on." I look to Remi. "We're ready, aren't we?"

"Yep. I can't believe you talked me into a PJ movie night, though."

"You have to admit, this is way more comfortable than those stilettos you wear to every party."

"Fine, but they aren't nearly as sexy." She wraps her arm around mine.

"Lills and Kyra meeting us here?"

"Yep, Kyra went to hang out with Ethan and Lillian."

I can't help but notice her frown. I'll have to make it a point to ask her how that's going the next chance I get.

Deghan weaves his fingers through mine on my free hand, a warm sensation I've grown fond of.

We enter the big open area which is now filled with blankets and couches and beanbags lined in rows. One of those fancy popcorn machines is near the entrance of the north wing, and the massive screen takes up the entire wall between the east and south sides.

Cameron waves us over to a spot on the west side, smiling and pointing to the seats he secured. Tons of pillows litter the floor, and a large couch is next to it.

He did well.

"What are we watching?" I settle into a spot on the floor.

Remi plops onto the couch, motioning with her hands in front of her. "*The. Princess. Bride.*" She enunciates each word one by one.

"Never seen it," I admit.

Cameron turns to me abruptly. "No way."

I smile. "I'm serious. Is it good?"

"So good, and seriously so perfect. It's—" He goes to speak but cuts himself off. "You'll see." He sits next to me, and Deghan plops down on the other side.

A few minutes into the trailers, Cam hops up and grabs us some popcorn. He hands us all our own bags and sits back down, closer to me than he had been.

I welcome him in with a nudge and scan the room, wondering where Kyra and Lillian are. I'm about to ask Remi when Ethan leads them in.

They take the seats next to Remi, and I relax back into mine.

It's not long before the popcorn is eaten and everyone gets cozy.

Cameron puts his arm around me and tugs me into him.

I allow my body to lean against him, soaking up his warmth.

Deghan ends up sprawling across the blanket, his head landing in my lap.

I run my fingers through his hair, and he purrs in response, nestling in more comfortably.

If only Sydney and Silas were here, but...they're both avoiding me, just in their own ways.

The next morning, I'm determined to talk to Sydney and figure out what's going on between us.

I knock on his door, shifting back to look in the hall, Deghan waiting near the entrance, trying to give me the distance I need without letting me too far out of his sight.

"Sydney, if you're in there, we need to talk." I pound again.

He doesn't answer, so I do something bold. I turn the handle and poke my head inside.

I scan the room, my gaze falling on his body, lying limp on his bed. I motion to Deghan with one finger, signaling I'll be right back. I step inside, tiptoeing my way toward him.

"Sydney!" I whisper-shout.

My heart picks up its pace, and worry courses through me.

Is he breathing?

I rush the rest of the way to the bed, studying his chest for the shallow rise and fall of life. I sigh in relief when it moves.

He must be exhausted if he's *this* out.

I brush a strand of his wavy hair off his forehead, admiring him while he sleeps. Not wanting to bother him anymore, I grab the notebook on his nightstand and write *We need to talk* and leave it there. I lean down, grazing my lips to his forehead, giving him one last look over and exiting the room.

Deghan meets me in the hallway. "So?"

I shrug. "He's knocked out. I left a note."

"Damn. Sorry, Wills. I know that's been bugging you."

"I don't get it. We were nearly inseparable...then he went all cold on me."

"Maybe it's for good reason," he suggests.

"Leave it to you to see the best in people."

"You should be glad. You looked like a mass murderer the first time I met you."

"It was raining." I push him, and he doesn't budge.

He's built like a brick house. Must be a werewolf thing.

Sydney manages to somehow *still* not find the time to come and talk to me, and the moment Monday morning rolls around, I'm furious.

Silas spent the whole evening being completely shut off, too, and having the both of them be this way is too much to handle.

Deghan escorts me to Walker's room, and ten minutes pass with no sign of Sydney.

Walker checks his watch for the umpteenth time. "He's not usually late."

I shake my head. I can't believe he's taken to *this* kind of extreme to avoid me. What gives him the right?

"Something must be wrong." Walker's salt-and-pepper brows furrow. "When was the last time you heard from him?"

I can't imagine something would be wrong, he's clearly just staying far away from me. "It's been days. Thursday. But I stopped by his room yesterday, and he was sleeping." Pretty damn soundly, though, if I remember correctly. What if I was foolish and something really had happened?

Without giving it another thought, I bolt from the headmaster's office, running across the foyer and up the north wing stairs. I don't knock, hoping the lack of privacy will be overlooked by my concern.

My heart seems to lurch from my chest as I take in the room.

Sydney somehow made it off his bed, the note I left him clinging in his hand, his body lying there awkwardly.

I rush to his side. "Oh god. Sydney." I put my hands on him, trying to locate the source of whatever is wrong. "Help!" I scream toward the door.

Walker rushes in, at my side, in an instant. A moment later, Silas appears behind me, wind whooshing in his wake.

"What's wrong with him?" I plead with Walker.

Silas's hands are on my shoulders, trying to pull me away to give Walker room.

The headmaster waves his hands over Sydney's body. "It...it appears his energy stores are dangerously low."

"What? How is that possible? What can we do?"

He lays Sydney flat on the floor, his palms stretched over him, focusing on some incantation.

I stare and stare, but Sydney doesn't move.

Panic consumes me, a strangely familiar feeling settling in my core. I rush to Sydney's other side, looking thoroughly at my hands.

*Don't fail me now,* I urge myself.

The faint glow of my magic surfaces, and I channel it forward.

Walker takes a small step back, giving me my own space this time, somehow trusting me when I'm totally unsure of what's about to happen.

Like a defibrillator, I rub my hands together, pressing them to Sydney's chest, willing my magic to exit my body and fill his.

His body rattles in response, confirming that I might be doing something right.

I repeat the same motions, shocking what I can of life back into his body. I do this again, and again, each time losing a little bit of hope that it's working. Tears well in my eyes.

"Willow," Walker says.

"I can do this," I cry.

I summon every single last ounce of my strength, sending a blast so fierce it rattles the walls, and finally, he sits straight up, gasping for air, wild-eyed but back here with us.

I pull him into a hug, nearly passing out from my own exhaustion, the adrenaline keeping me upright.

It's not until his arms wrap around me that I can take a breath of my own.

"You came for me," he breathes into my hair.

"I'm so sorry," is all I can say.

# CHAPTER 15

Wednesday rolls around, and things sort of go back to normal.

Sydney is still acting strange, but he's choosing to do so around me, and not ignore me completely. It's off-putting but better than the alternative.

I haven't quite shaken the feeling that he's hiding something, and the fear of not knowing what happened to him still rocks me to my core.

He had no answer. No explanation, other than he overexerted himself.

Walker told me it's possible, but unlikely, which throws me off even more.

"Are you excited?" Deghan smiles brightly. He's standing in

the foyer where we're all anxiously awaiting our people for family day.

Walker, Abigail, and Professor Tremont are outside, maintaining the security of the grounds and scanning the arrivals, allowing them entry. They do so in such a discreet manner that it doesn't cause concern from the non-supernaturals.

Remi, Kyra, Lillian, and Ethan stand off to the side. Remi gives me a quick wave from across the room.

A gorgeous middle-aged couple walks in and heads straight to her. She beams and jumps into what I assume are her father's broad arms.

Cameron's brother is the first of our small group to arrive. He comes through the entryway and clasps onto Cam's shoulders, pulling him in for a bear hug.

"Guys, this is Austin. Austin, this is Deghan, Sydney, and Willow."

I take his hand into mine and shake it firmly.

Austin's eyes widen, and he looks to Cam in surprise. "Did he hire you to pretend to be his friend?" He laughs and smacks Cam.

I clear my throat, not totally liking his comment. "If anything, I'm the one lucky he's friends with me."

"Wow, he totally paid you off."

I narrow my eyes.

"See you later?" Cam shifts his gaze between us.

I nod. "Yeah."

The two of them leave, and we wait for whoever is next.

I secretly hope it's Mom and Uncle Danny. I've missed them both so damn much. Not to mention those blueberry muffins that my mom makes are my favorite.

I glance over. Kyra and Remi are gone now, leaving Ethan and Lillian.

An uptight blonde woman strolls in, taking her sunglasses off and placing them on her head. She scans the room and settles on her target. I follow her line of sight, Allie in her path.

"Maybe that's why Allie is always in a bad mood." Deghan throws a thumb in their direction.

"Could be," I mutter, my gaze going right back to the door.

A beautiful woman with dark hair, a pencil skirt, and an over-priced bag glides in next, her gaze focusing in our direction.

Sydney takes in a breath like he's holding it. "Mom," he says finally, forcing a smile.

She comes toward us, not bothering to embrace her son in a way that moms typically do. She looks down her nose at me in pure disgust and says, "Come along now," to Sydney.

"Sorry," he mouths, dread apparent on his face.

No wonder he had a crappy childhood, his mother is Cruella de Vil. Plus, something felt very *off* about her. An unsettling pit opens up inside me.

Deghan goes to grab my hand but then lets go. "Sorry, I'm nervous."

I wrap my arm around his, gripping him tightly to my side. "Me, too."

A few people come in, finding their students and going off on their way. Some of them stop in front of Lills, leading her and Ethan away.

I glance at the clock, noting the twenty minutes that's gone by.

My mom and Danny are very aware of how much I'm a stickler for time, so the fact that they're late is strange.

An older gentleman strolls in, and Deghan shifts his weight, a smile spreading across his face.

"Degs," the man calls out with his arms outstretched.

"Uncle Rollin, you made it." Deghan releases my arm, yanking his uncle in for a hug. "Where's Aunt Cass?"

"Busy, you know how she is." Rollin elbows his nephew. "And who's this?"

"Uncle Rollin, this is Willow Oliver."

I extend my hand, and he swats it away, hugging me instead. I can't help but smile, his action reminding me heavily of Deghan.

I shift back to the door, and the happiness fades.

"I can stay and wait with you," Deghan offers.

"No, they're only running a minute late. You two go ahead, enjoy your day. I'll catch up to you." I push Deghan toward his uncle, faking a smile. "Don't worry."

Rollin punches Deghan's shoulder playfully. "Show me where the snacks are."

I turn, letting them do their thing, not wanting to draw any more sympathy from Deghan. I continue to stand there until the last student files away with their person. I check the time, forty-five minutes past. I sigh, settling into the nearest chair, a clear line of sight to the door.

A few more minutes pass, and the door opens. I sit upright, only to be disappointed by Walker entering the building.

Before he latches his eyes on to me, I click myself invisible, a lone tear rolling down my cheek.

*"You are nothing,"* the voice commands. *"They forgot about you...or worse, they didn't want to come at all."*

I dig my nails into my palm, desperate to feel anything other than what I'm feeling.

*"This is how you'll end up. Alone. Forgotten."*

I shake my head, more tears spilling down.

*"No wonder your father left. You deserve to lose everyone."*

I force myself to stand, turning on my heel and slamming straight into Silas. My invisible form melts into him.

"How did you...?" I blubber.

He wraps his arms around me, despite not being able to even see where I begin or end. He presses me into him, rubbing his hands along my shoulders and back. "Come on." He leads me toward the stairs, down the hall, and into his dorm. Closing the door behind him, he reaches into my hand, somehow finding the pen. He takes my hand and places his on top, clicking the button and bringing me back.

With his thumbs, he swipes away the rogue tears on my cheeks and pulls me in again.

"Don't you…have people coming?" I manage.

He shakes his head. "No."

"Are they busy or something?"

He sighs. "It's just me."

At his admission, I squeeze him more, my hands desperate to find some new level of closeness that will erase the brokenness between us. I recall the moment in the woods when he told me his greatest fear was being forgotten. This only solidifies his meaning behind that so much more.

"I'm sorry," I say.

"Shh." He lifts me off the floor slightly, gliding over to his bed. He nudges me down, under the blanket, coming in once I'm situated. Silas grabs something off his nightstand, pushing a switch, and the lights shut off, leaving us in complete darkness. "Tell me if it's too much."

"It's perfect." I relax my body into his, still recovering from the hiccupping tears.

He slides his arm under my head, the other along my stomach. "I don't sleep that much, but if I do, it has to be really dark." He positions his body firmly around mine, fitting us together like two puzzle pieces.

It's a calming comfort I didn't know was possible.

I close my eyes, holding on tight, too afraid to let go, allowing his presence to rid me of my demons.

***

Once the tremors stop and I'm soothed back to my senses, I roll over, facing Silas in the dark.

"You must think I'm crazy." My voice is a faint wisp in the utter silence of the room.

He brushes his hand over my face, enveloping it with his palm. "Not at all."

"Why are you doing this?"

"It kills me that you're hurting. If I can help a little, I'd do anything to ease your pain."

I want to ask him why he pulls away, why he becomes so distant and reclusive, why he's hurting so much and won't tell me why…but there's such uncertainty of whether that will push him that much further, and that alone glues my mouth shut. There is *something* strong between us, and with that, there's this terrifying doom threatening to tear us apart. The thought of being the reason he's not around is enough to have me walking on eggshells.

I have to learn more about our connection and to uncover his hidden layers, but I have to do it carefully.

I sit up, the realization only now hitting me. How could I be so stupid? The voice in my head tricked me into thinking my mom and Uncle Danny didn't come because they didn't want to, but maybe it was because of something else?

"What's going on in that head of yours?" Silas repositions himself, his hand rubbing circles on my back.

"What if something is wrong?"

"With your mom?"

"Yeah." I jump out of bed, throwing the covers off and bumping straight into a hard object. "Shit. Can you get the lights?"

Barely a second goes by, and the room brightens.

I shield my eyes, noting the shelf full of books I stubbed my toe on. "You read?"

Silas chuckles, "Mmhm."

My gaze is drawn to a few of my most beloved titles. "You've read *The Sandman's Travel*?"

"One of my favorites," he confirms.

"I've never met a single person who knows that book exists."

"Have you read *Henry's Redemption*?" Silas slides his shoes on.

"Are you kidding me? Probably half a dozen times."

He strides up behind me, resting his face against my hair,

scanning the contents of the shelf with me. He swipes my hair off my shoulder tenderly. "What about *Faraway Nothing*?"

I shake my head.

Plucking it off the shelf, he hands me the old, tattered book. "First edition," he clarifies. "I think you'll love it."

"Thank you." I smile.

His hand stays on top of mine, and our eyes meet. He's so goddamn gorgeous it blows my mind.

"Now," he changes the subject, "you should call your mom, make sure everything is okay."

I nod. "Yeah."

"There has to be a reason she didn't show." He takes my hand, leading me toward the door.

We arrive in the foyer. What I assume to be a mom and a dad walk to stand next to their daughter near the garden. They point inside, clearly gawking at the beauty of the design.

Silas knocks on Headmaster Walker's office door. A moment goes by with no answer. He grips the handle, poking his head inside. "He's not here," he mutters.

"He probably wouldn't mind, right?" I shrug, stepping inside anyway. I make my way around the side of his desk, clutching the phone off its charger, dialing the number.

It rings a few times and goes to voicemail.

I sigh, hitting redial and listening to the tone again.

On the third ring, an out-of-breath Danny answers. "Hello?"

"Danny, hey. Are you okay?"

Relief and concern flood through me at the same time. He's on the other end, he's alive, but he's panting.

"Yeah, sorry. I was in the shower. I had to run down the stairs to answer." He exhales deeply. "Are you okay? What's wrong?"

"Um, well, you and Mom were supposed to be here for family day. I talked to her last week, and she said you were off work. I thought something had happened." At least his windedness is for a good reason.

"Oh no, I had no idea. When was it?" His voice seems sincere.

"Today."

"Crap, Willow. I'm so sorry. I had no idea. Your mom, she didn't tell me."

"It's okay. Can I talk to her?"

"I'd let ya, but she's not here. She left a note saying she was going to be staying with her friend. Said Jenny was going to pick her up and take her to some girls' retreat. She had a letter from her doctor and everything. She's been doing a lot better, by the way. I've been surprised. She's damn near back to the woman I knew from a long time ago. Blows my mind. You'd be proud of her progress."

I swallow, fear creeping heavily back in.

Silas stands alert next to me, the dread rolling its way through him.

"Thanks, Danny." My voice shakes. "I'll talk to you later."

"Okay, Wills. I'm really sorry about today. Tell me how I can make it up to you."

I cut him off. "It's all right. Bye." I hang up without letting him respond.

"I don't understand," Silas scans me. "Danny is okay. Your mom is with her friend. Yeah, it sucks that she left you hanging, but they're both fine, and your mom seems to be doing better. What's wrong?"

I put the phone back on the receiver, and it clinks into place. Stalking to the door, I process the conversation, analyzing and picking it apart. How can this be possible?

"Talk to me, please," he begs.

I turn to face him, my attention shifting from the floor to lock onto his eyes.

"My mom's friend Jenny..." My gaze goes blank and I try to make sense of it.

He waits patiently for a response.

"Silas...she's dead. We went to her funeral a few years back." I shake my head, the tears threatening their way to the front. I'm so fucking sick of crying that it fuels the rage within me even more. "She's gone. I have no idea where my mother is. And I have no idea how to find her."

# CHAPTER 16

"It's too dangerous, you can't leave," Headmaster Walker insists. "I can't allow you to put your life at risk like that, especially with no idea of her whereabouts."

"How do you expect me to sit here and do *nothing*? My mother is missing."

He holds out his hand. "I understand, Willow, but acting irrationally isn't going to bring her back. If you didn't have an unknown curse, I would still advise you against it. Listen, I can help." He motions around the space. "We can help. I have a team of locators I can send out to track your mom. Do you have any of her belongings here at the school? That will help with their search."

I exhale loudly. "Yeah. In my dorm. A necklace she gave me."

"That's perfect. Now," his voice gets calm, "we need a little time. We'll find her."

"And I'm supposed to do what exactly in the meantime?" I don't mean for my words to come across as harsh as they do.

"You have more than your fair share of work cut out for yourself. I encourage you to focus on your research, your schooling. You don't have to do it all on your own. This is one of those things better suited for someone else to handle."

He's not wrong, but damn does it suck to have to sit on the sidelines and do nothing while my mom is out there *somewhere*. My main saving grace is knowing that her magic is back, that she's in her right-ish mind and in control of herself.

"I have a group on the way to your house right now to check things out. I assure you, we will locate her."

I leave his office, stunned and in disbelief of what my life is coming to.

I only just found out that my father might exist, and here I am, losing my mother.

"You should eat," Silas suggests.

He weaves his hand through mine, a shock coursing through me at the very public show of affection.

His embrace is comforting, despite the unsettling chill in my body.

"I'm not hungry."

"It's not an option."

A family walks by us, and it's all I can do to not let go of his hand and take off, running far away from here.

"We'll get something and take it up to the room." His hand reassuringly grips mine.

"Okay."

We head to the dining hall, Silas acquiring our food while I numbly walk beside him.

He fills the sack, and without speaking to another soul, I follow him out.

Making a left and up the stairs to the west wing, we go to my dorm.

"Do you want to tell the guys what's going on?" he asks.

I shake my head. "Not now. I'll let them enjoy their day." I'm the constant bearer of bad news. I'll give them another few hours.

Ten minutes pass.

"Will you at least eat this?" Silas holds out a rather large brownie.

I stop pushing the salad around in my bowl and put the fork down. I eyeball his offering, then Silas.

"Remember what happened last time?" His gorgeous gray eyes plead with me.

"Fine." I take it reluctantly and bite into the delicious choco-latiness.

He smirks and then takes a mouthful of his burger.

"You probably didn't expect to be stuck with me all day." I lean back against the oversized windowsill seat where we sit, eating our food.

"You act as though I'd rather be doing something else."

"Would you?"

"What do you think?" He raises an eyebrow, and for a split second, I forget all my worries.

But only for the smallest moment.

"Do you mind if we go to the library when we're done?" Part of me would rather stay in my dorm all day, alone with him, but considering how *fucked* my life is, I won't be able to focus on anything other than the constant problems I can't seem to solve. If anything, centering my thoughts on the curse will keep me from the constant worry of my mom.

"I'd love to."

---

For some reason, the longer I spend in the library, the more I pace. I find a book, open it up, make zero sense of what I'm reading, and then walk circles around the room. It's an annoying habit I've developed.

"You exert more energy that way, you realize that, right?" Silas looks up from his own studies to watch me with concerned eyes.

I set the book down on the table. "What do you know about angels...and witches?"

He tilts his head like he's recalling a memory. "Legends have it that witches were descended from angels. At least very few of them. The rest were created by Mother Nature...the gods...the Devil...so on. But in time, they all sort of mixed together and became one. Now, no one can really pinpoint where they originated from. Why?"

"These wings." I poke at them on the page. "I've seen them countless times. In these texts, in real life..."

"I don't see anything."

"Right here," I insist, furiously digging my finger at the spot.

He shakes his head. "Describe them to me."

"They're white, flowy, heavenly, powdery, and definitely two big-ass beautiful wings."

"That's the mark of the angel." He meets my gaze.

"I wonder what it means."

He laughs, catching me off guard.

"Oh, it makes perfect sense," he adds.

"What does?"

"Willow." Silas lays his hand on top of mine. "You have angel blood running through your veins."

"I do?" I stare at him.

"It's no wonder your family was oppressed. If this is true, you're pretty much *the* royal witch family."

"You're joking?"

His face is nothing but serious, despite how insane the words coming out of his mouth are. "No." He pauses. "Listen, this is dangerous information. You need to be careful with who you tell."

Something inside me flickers, setting me on edge.

"Willow."

I nearly jump at his voice.

"Mr. Walker, sorry, you startled me." I clutch at my chest. "Did you find anything?"

"Yes and no."

"Okay..." I wait for him to elaborate.

He stands in the doorway. "The house was scanned, and there were no reports of lingering demonic energy. I called in a hand-writing analyst to check the note your mom left. The results were conclusive to support the idea that your mom departed on her own free will."

If she chose to leave, why would she have lied and said she was going with Jenny? Especially considering we went to Jenny's funeral. The two of them went to high school together, and she was torn up about her loss, so to nonchalantly bring it up now is that much weirder. Why wouldn't she have called and told me she was leaving and not lead me to believe she would come to family day?

All of this doesn't add up.

"And what about tracking?" I say.

"We're still working on it. I'll keep you posted if anything changes." He motions to the book splayed out on the table. "Making any progress?"

Silas's words pound through my head, *"Be careful."* His stare burns a hole through me.

"No." I sigh.

"Keep at it. I'm sure you'll figure it out."

I force a smile, nodding and watching him dismiss himself.

Lying isn't something I'm proud of, but not knowing what any of this means and *feeling* the concern Silas had when he told me to be cautious zips my mouth shut. But how can I be so sure that Silas is trustworthy, too?

"It's only until we can figure out what to do with the infor-mation," Silas says tenderly.

"And what if we never do?"

"We will. But until then, you have to keep this between us."

"What about Sydney?"

"Especially him. He's a LeBlanc, Willow. Nothing good comes out of that family." Silas's jaw clenches, his energy thrumming.

"Tell me about them?"

"Where to start...they're greedy, self-serving narcissists."

The room thickens with his emotion.

"Hey." I take his hand in mine. "I won't say anything, okay?" I do what I can to push into him my calming aura. A glimmer of pink and purple floats around us, illuminating the area.

Silas's stone face softens. His gaze shifts around the room to the light show, settling back on me. "You'll never see yourself how I do, and that is a damn shame."

***

The families leave for the day, and Silas and I find the guys, filling them in on what's happened.

"Damn, it keeps getting worse for you, doesn't it?" Deghan frowns and extends his arms, doing his best to hug away the stupid shit going wrong in my life.

Sydney rubs his chin. "Abigail has a natural locating ability, but she learned from the best. Walker has a lot of resources he can pull from. They'll find her in no time."

"What can I do to help?" Cam asks.

"Unless you have any idea where my mom would have gone..." The idea strikes me, and I can't believe I hadn't thought of it earlier. "My dad."

"You think she went in search of your dad?" Sydney straightens.

"Has to be. She was so excited when I went to her house and spoke to her about everything that happened. With the love curse broken, she could finally get him back. It's either that or a demon kidnapped her and is holding her ransom, which isn't a far-fetched idea now that I say it out loud."

"I thought you said Walker ruled that out?" Cameron confirms.

I nod. "Yeah, so he thought, but you never know. Could have been a witch who took her." My gaze shifts to Sydney and back to the floor.

*"How can you trust any of them?"* the voice taunts.

I stare at my hands, totally caught off guard by the intrusion but not wanting to show the vulnerability to the guys. The thing in my head is typically at bay if they're around, but for some reason, it's louder than ever, concerning me that maybe their presence no longer has a protective type of effect.

*"Or maybe, one of them is the reason all of this is happening."*

"You okay, Wills?" Deghan questions, his brows furrowed.

"I think I need to be alone for a little while." I don't dare allow my eyes to wander to them.

A flush of sadness mixed with desperation fills the room, funneling out of each one of them, me included.

"Of course," one of them mutters.

A large warm hand touches my shoulder. *Deghan.*

Footsteps wander to the door.

"I'll be right outside if you need me." Silas floats across the room and then disappears.

They all do.

They're gone.

And I'm left alone, but not truly, the evil version of myself to keep me company.

I curl into a ball on my bed, on top of the covers, silence filling the space. I grip each shoulder with the opposite hand and squeeze tight, hopeful to force a fraction of the calming relief into me that I can for others.

I fail, limbs going slack, and allow the sadness to take hold. My mind is a danger I'm not sure how to handle, but how can I ask for help not knowing who to trust?

# CHAPTER 17

Two weeks pass with no solid leads on my mother's whereabouts.

The trackers follow a path, only to hit dead end followed by dead end.

I can't be of any service, not having a clue what my father's name is or where a single one of his possessions are located.

Uncle Danny is no help either, although he's filed an official missing person's report. Not that the Harper County Sheriff's office will be of much assistance, given the most severe case they've ever dealt with was the local seniors toilet papering the high school one year.

I find the thoughts in my head to be all-consuming. I can no longer differentiate which are mine anymore, and that alone terrifies me. I'm in too deep, and as much as I struggle, I can't find my way out.

I spend less time with the guys, or, well, I speak to them less. I don't really talk much at all, to anyone. They're there, watching over me always, but I've become reclusive, folding into myself. I spend my days studying, either school or magic things, and trying to sleep. It's a fruitless task for the most part, but people don't seem to want to pry if you're trying to rest, so I use the excuse any chance I can.

I force moments with the girls, although I'm shit company. But I can't imagine losing them again, so I do the minimum without losing too much.

Somehow, I pass all of my exams with flying colors. I guess I really was excelling in my classes like Walker had said. My accounting class took the brunt of my regular school attention with those annoying balance sheets and income statements. The creative writing essay was a breeze. We had to pick a fictional character we admire and explain why. My choice was easy, Rudy from *The Sandman's Travel*. His grit and determination to overcome every insane hurdle that life threw at him was admirable. He loved so deeply and never once gave up, even when anyone else would have. That was one assignment I actually looked forward to doing.

Being so new to the magical world, I never had any solidified supernatural classes or final exams. Next term will be a different story, though, depending on whether or not we can fix the shadow realm.

Each day Walker reassures me that he and his team are *doing their best* to find my mom, but I can't help but think *I* should be the one out there looking for her. It only throws me that much farther down the rabbit hole I'm stuck in.

Abigail told me she thinks my mother's magic is hidden similar to how mine is, protecting us from the wrong people finding us. "I'm a firm believer in intuition, Willow. We're going to find her."

"How can you be so sure?" I asked, hopelessness consuming me.

"Trust me."

That word I keep circling back to. *Trust.* How can I know for certain that any of them have my best interests in mind? Especially given people are notorious for being self-serving. Sure, intuition may be a good judge, but what do I do with the gut feeling that *something* isn't what it seems. *Someone* is lying, and I have no idea who or what about.

Maybe it's me. Maybe I'm the one allowing my mind to play tricks on me. But what if I'm wrong, what if it's those I care about most, deceiving me in the worst of ways?

How can I trust myself?

"Sydney is going to be taking over soon. Do you need anything before I leave?" Cameron asks, his voice soft like he's walking on eggshells.

I force a smile. "No, thank you, though."

He sits next to me in the large windowsill seat in my dorm room. "You're worrying me, Willow. You remind me of a zombie. You barely eat or drink anything, other than coffee. You haven't spoken but a few words to me in all of two weeks. I'm not trying to pry. I really hope you understand I'm here for you if you want to talk. I'm not *all-mighty and powerful* in some fancy supernatural way like the other guys, but I swear to you, I'm the best listener ever." He sighs, putting a hand on my knee. "I care about you; do you realize that?"

I give my focus to him and nod. "I do. I'm sorry I'm...*this way.*"

"No, no, no, that's not what I meant. There is nothing wrong with you. This is hard on all of us, too. Not having any idea of how to help is brutal."

The bedroom door creaks open, and Sydney walks in. He sets his bag on the closest bed and takes out whatever he's working on today. Without saying a word to either of us, he digs into his book.

Cameron gives my leg a gentle squeeze. "We're going to get through this, okay?"

"Yeah," I whisper, damn well hoping he's right.

Cam leaves, and I move toward the window, scanning the grounds for a familiar face.

I locate Deghan a moment later, staring straight toward the setting night sky, the purple-and-orange horizon casting colorful shadows across him.

I summon the pink ball into my hand, tenderly tossing it out the window, following it along on its way down to him.

He adjusts, letting it flow through him, and turns around. He motions for me to come down and frowns at my shaking head.

"Are you going to work on anything tonight?" Sydney asks.

I shrug.

"I brought you a few books."

I glance at his bag, walking over to check out the contents. "I'm kind of tired. I might try to nap."

He rolls his eyes. "What would you rather be doing?"

"Something other than sitting in this school doing *nothing*."

Sydney rubs his temples. "I think I might be able to help. Do you still have that pen?"

I grab it out of my pocket a second later and extend it out to him.

"Good. Now, pack a bag."

My eyes go wide. "Are we leaving?"

"Keep your voice down. But yes. Bring whatever you need. I know how we can find your mom." He shoves the books in his backpack. "Go."

A few minutes later, we're holding hands, invisible, and tiptoeing down the west wing stairs. We clear the garden, stopping dead in our tracks when Silas walks by.

He halts, scanning the area. "Willow," he mouths.

I hold my breath, the grip I have on Sydney's hand growing tighter.

Silas moves on, jogging up the north steps and out of sight.

"We have to move," Sydney urges quietly.

I settle into the passenger seat and let out a heavy exhale. "That was intense."

Sydney turns the key, the engine of his car roaring to life. In a hurry, he puts the vehicle in drive and speeds out of the parking lot without anyone seeing us.

We turn off the gravel drive, and the security of the school is left behind. A strange vulnerability pulses through me. I push it aside, letting the freedom of finally getting to do something productive come to the forefront.

Sydney white knuckles the steering wheel. "It's not too far."

"What isn't?"

"My house."

"We're going to your house?" I hope this isn't a gigantic mistake, but what could be the harm in going to his home?

"Our family...we have a vast collection of magical devices. There's a stone that can help us locate your mother."

His words register, but I don't quite understand the hesitation behind them.

"And you're just now telling me this?" It's everything I can do to not get mad at him for hiding such a thing from me for all this time.

"You don't get it, Willow." He glances at me. "My parents... they'll probably disown me for this."

"Sydney." I grasp his arm. "We don't have to do this. We can figure out another way."

"I can't stand to see you this way anymore. It's killing me. It's torturing all of us. And here I am with a way to help and I haven't. I'm so sorry." His jaw clenches.

I scan his face, eyeing the stubble he's let grow out a little in the last week. His minty-green eyes are filled with longing and despair.

"For what it's worth, thank you for changing your mind. But if you want to go back to school, we can." Deep down, I beg that he stays the course.

"That will be another battle we face."

"Walker is going to kill us himself."

The headmaster has tirelessly secured the school to protect us, developed teams to try to locate my mom, and has been working to repair the shadow realm, and here we are, sneaking out and putting ourselves in danger.

Sydney turns the car into a long gravel lane. Two large stone pillars sit off the road, leading to what seems to be nothing.

"How long is your driveway?"

"About a mile," he says.

A pit unravels in my stomach the farther we go.

The house comes into sight, my jaw dropping in response.

"You live in a mansion?" I roll my gaze over the vast architecture. It may be dark, but I can still make out the intricately laid stone face and three massive levels. Sharply landscaped square bushes line the front of the house, an archway at the entrance, inviting us in.

"My parents do. I live over there." He points toward a smaller but still expansive building off to the right.

"In the guest house?" I can't hide the surprise in my voice.

Sydney puts the car in park, getting out and coming over to open my door. He takes my hand into his, leading me toward his place. "I want you to wait in here while I go in the house and find the reperio stone."

"You're going to leave me?" I latch on to his arm.

"Not for long. Only to get what we need. My parents are really weird about who's in the house...I don't want to set off any alarms by bringing someone they didn't invite in."

"You're right, that is weird."

He opens the door, and we enter his home.

It smells so...Sydney. Earth and wind wrapped up in one, dipped in honey and coffee.

I let my eyes adjust to the studio-style room. A vast book collection lines two walls in the back, and across from that is a king-sized bed and desk area. A full-sized kitchen sits in another corner, various doors lining the wall.

"Bathroom is over there if you need it." He points to one of them. "I'll be right back." Sydney hesitates, running a finger along my arm. He leans in, pressing his lips to my cheek. "Make yourself at home."

I plop down on the dark-brown couch and sink into the seat, my feet dangling, barely off the floor. I glance around, not trying to invade Sydney's privacy but wanting to occupy my time.

*"He's not coming back."*

"Stop talking," I mutter to myself.

*"You realize this is a trap, right?"*

My heart thuds. That can't possibly be true. I shake my head.

*"Why do you think he left? You really are such a fool."*

"He's trying to help me," I demand.

*"Is that what you think? He doesn't care about you. Why do you think he went without you? You bought right into his lies."*

"Sydney hasn't lied to me. You don't know what you're talking about."

*"You'll find out soon enough, especially if you stay sitting like a duck."*

What if the voice is right? What if this really is a trick and I'm falling right for it? But what could Sydney possibly have to gain?

That's the moment it dawns on me.

Silas's words, *He's a LeBlanc, Willow. Nothing good comes out of that family.*

Maybe Sydney really is the bad guy.

I jump up, surveying the room, not having any luck finding what I'm looking for. I rummage through Sydney's bag, no cell phone in sight.

*Shit.*

*"You better hurry if you want to make it out."*

"What, so now you're suddenly on my side?"

I shift my focus up to the main house, watching as a light flickers on in a window at the far end. If I act now, I can get out without him catching me. The school isn't *that* far away, I could easily run all the way back there and beg Headmaster Walker to let me in. He's a reasonable man, and I'm willing to take whatever punishment he sees fit.

Clutching the bag in my hands, I make for the door. I slip outside quietly, plotting my escape on the way.

*"Go through the woods, it'll be a more direct path to the school."*

I sigh. That *is* the direction the school is in, but should I really trust the voice in my head? Out of the corner of my eye, the house goes dark, and I know for sure if I'm going to leave, I have to do it now. Without another thought, I make a beeline straight through the yard, past Sydney's car, and into the wooded area surrounding his house.

# CHAPTER 18

I was a fool for ever considering leaving the safety of the school. Why was I so stupid and careless? I left the protection Walker worked so hard on, and now here I am, running nearly blind through a dark thickly wooded forest with no real sense of direction.

I make a path through the area for nearly five minutes, only going deeper and deeper into the forest, no roads or trails in sight. I slow to a jog and then stop, placing my hands on my knees to catch my breath for a second. I shift my head around.

"Where the hell am I?" I squint.

A laugh fills my head. *"Foolish girl."* The voice is evil and taunting. The scariest part about it is how similar it sounds to my own. The voice calls out, *"Right behind you."*

I turn around in a hurry, only to find nothing but the dark night sky funneling through the cracks in the trees.

*"To your left."*

I jump again.

*"To your right, no, there!"*

I stop spinning around in circles, only realizing too late that the voice in my head is trying to disorient me. And it completely works.

"Was this even a trap?" I insist, rage fueling me at being so easily duped.

*"In due time, Willow."*

I take a step forward, determined to find the way to my temporary home.

*"Are you sure about that?"*

I stop, glancing around, nothing really showing me which way to go. I close my eyes, pulling my magic toward me in an all too familiar way. "Which way?" I mouth.

The energy bubbles up, and right when it's about to answer, the voice interrupts.

*"It's such a shame you've ended up alone. But it's not really all that surprising, is it? Deep down, you knew you'd drive everyone away. You're nothing. No wonder no one wants anything to do with you. You're a waste of space, a disgrace to your name. You don't deserve the power surging through your veins. Those friends of yours, they're going to forget you without you having to take their memories. They'll do it without your help because you're that forgettable. Brooke is moving on without a second thought, like you worried she would. And the guys, oh, you thought they cared about you? How pathetic are you? Each one of them was using you for something. They're all better off without you. Why do you think your dad left, why your mother abandoned you? You're an embarrassment. Even your Uncle Danny can't be bothered to show up. This world would be a better place if you had never been born. You should do everyone a kindness and be gone."*

Each word stings more than the next. They tear down my

defenses, break me in ways I never imagined, and there's not a fucking thing I can do to make them stop. At some point, I fall to my knees, my hands digging into the dirt around me. A sad pathetic waste of a witch.

My heart aches. My soul crushed. My magic a faraway thing I can't seem to summon despite desperately trying.

A flash of light bursts about a dozen feet in front of me, and for the smallest second, my mom stands there.

I'm on my feet in a rush, half stumbling and running toward the light.

It disappears, along with the beautiful woman.

I crash into the ground, my knees scraping forcibly, skin ripping away and stinging badly. Somehow, it's nothing compared to the wound inside my chest.

*"If anything, I give you credit for making my job that much easier."*

The earth around me shakes, a crack forming a few feet away, a deep, dark-red illumination pooling out. A type of fog seeps through, twisting and turning and swirling up and out, forming into a creature above the surface.

Another demon.

*"You see, it was so simple, luring you out into the woods. You practically walked yourself right onto a bull's-eye. It might as well be taking candy from a baby."*

Another flash, and this time there's Lillian, her face contorted and strained. I launch straight toward her, my arms slashing through at nothing, and she disappears into thin air.

*"See, I told you."*

I blink through the haze, trying to figure out what's real and what isn't.

The long and lanky demon that shaped itself from a strange dark smog definitely appears real. It turns toward me, and I stumble back, grating my hands on the rocks lining the ground behind me.

Something resembling a nose sniffs the air as though it's

smelling the blood seeping from my wounds. A long, lizard-like tongue licks its lipless face, and the demon hovers toward me.

I kick at it, the demon shifting its body to block the blow and reforming immediately. Unlike the last demon I faced, this one doesn't speak.

*"It doesn't need to. I do all the talking for it, and I control its every move. The only reason it hasn't attacked is because I haven't allowed it to."*

"What are you waiting for?" The words remind me of sticky peanut butter in my mouth. My speech slurs, and my hearing changes. These *things* can control how I see and think and speak, and they're suppressing my magic. I really did walk right into this trap, and there is no way out.

If that's the case, maybe Sydney isn't against me in some way. Unfortunately, staring into the face of this demon, being completely stripped of all my abilities, I'll never know the truth.

*"I'm going to enjoy this, watching you squirm and suffer. No one is coming for you, Willow. You're mine now to do with as I please."*

The demon floats closer, and I inch back more, this time slamming into a tree, halted to a complete stop.

The dark hazy creature grazes my foot, and a surge of power exits my body, leaving me even more weak and helpless.

I swallow down the reality that I'm going to die out here in these woods, alone and confused about what's real or not. At the end of the day, this is all my fault. My fault for thinking I could challenge the curse, that I could overcome it and free the Olivers of their oppression. That I could ever have people in my life who cared about me and that I would get to experience what love felt like. I should have never left the school. And more, I never should have thought I could have a new start at the academy. If I stayed home, none of this ever would have happened. I wouldn't have hurt people who never deserved to be hurt. I never would have lost my mom.

*"Yes, Willow. You're exactly right. Now, you finally see how much of a burden you are."*

Another flicker, Silas appearing, concern lining every perfect inch of his face. But this time, I don't move. It's fake, some ruse to get me to move forward, and for once, I don't allow it to happen. I'm done playing this thing's games. If it wants me, it's going to have to come get me itself.

Reading my mind, the voice laughs and commands the dark haze toward me. The pain is sharp and bitter when it caresses my legs, inching up my body. I lose focus on the vision of Silas, the hot agony forcing my eyes shut.

If anything, at least the last thing I'll have seen before I die is the face of someone I care about deeply.

"Willow," Silas's speech fills my ears. He winces, a yelp of pain leaving his mouth.

I must be delirious, or the voice is now attacking me with a new tactic.

Hands grip my shoulders, shaking me fiercely. They're cool and strong and rattle me with the energy that pulses through them and into me. Hands all too memorable. Hands that could truly only belong to one person.

"Silas," I breathe.

He pulls me away from the tree, setting me right back down only a few feet away but removing me from the spot where the demon remains.

I open my eyes and find him standing in front of me, shielding me with himself, blocking the demon with his beautiful purple magic. He whips his arm back like a baseball pitcher, a ball of glowing power forming and being expelled in the direction of the demon.

A portion of the creature falls apart, and it quickly retreats to the crevice, only to be reformed by more dark fog.

"It's regenerating," I say.

"Willow, stay behind me." Silas plants his feet, standing firmly in place.

I stand, somehow finding my strength in his presence. Stumbling, I find my own footing next to him. "Do you mind?" I hold out my hand next to his shoulder.

He nods his approval, and I place my hand on him, soaking up some of his strength.

I'm not even sure how I knew that would work, but feeling his hands on me a few moments earlier, I realize Silas breathes a whole new life into me that I was so unaware of.

I let go of him, the wave of energy soaring back through me.

*"You're smart, but not smart enough."* The terror in its voice sends chills up my spine.

The demon settles to the ground, splitting into dozens of other human-sized versions of itself. They stop multiplying, only to shift their form further, taking on the identity of the person who stands right next to me.

Without allowing him to protest, I summon my energy, placing both hands on him. "You have to go. I'll be okay. I promise."

Silas's eyes go wide, but I don't let it change my mind. I shove a burst of magic into him, willing him as far as I can push him into the forest.

"I can't hurt you if you're not here," I say into the darkness.

I turn back to the strange hell, dozens of angry Silas's stalking toward me.

One by one, they attack. Swift and violent but no match to my power. It's not long until they come in packs, and then, all at once.

Each defeated Silas is a punch to my gut, reminding me over and over of something I'm incredibly afraid of. Thinking I had killed him a few weeks back was nearly the end of me—it shattered the shadow realm and fractured my soul. I will never allow that to happen again, and that's exactly why I sent him away, knowing my magic is what has to bring this monster down.

I scream, but this time, no sudden atomic bomb of energy,

just pure, unadulterated rage with every ball of power, ripping each Silas apart piece by piece.

Minutes, maybe hours go by, and I'm lost in a fury of swinging my arms, throwing magic at each thing coming my way.

The fake Silases keep coming, and for a second it crosses my mind that I'm not sure how long I can keep going. It's a fleeting thought, though, and is replaced with the endless desire to keep those I care about safe.

I blast another Silas in half, ripping him to shreds and focusing on another. The shattered remains drift down and then dissipate completely.

A dozen of them run toward me, and I heave my magic in, reeling it to a concentrated core, waiting for the right moment to fire it, blowing them all away and preparing for the next attack.

The demons' spawning rate decreases, and for once, there's a manageable number of Silases to destroy.

My vision moves me to something else, a new face in the crowd.

*Sydney.*

But this apparition doesn't flash, doesn't have a weird white light like the others. It doesn't attack, it merely hovers on the ground near the crack in the earth where the demons keep coming from.

Sydney waves his arms, his mouth moving, and jolts of green magic flow into the ground. His face is tight and serious.

A Silas blurs in my peripheral, and I slash at it, sending it back to whatever hell it came from. I throw a dagger of flowing pink magic at two more, then rotate and hit three.

I spin in a circle slowly, counting the six left that surround me.

At once, they raise their hands, coming at me slower than they ever have.

"Willow," they say in unison, a voice so similar to the real Silas.

This new tactic throws me a wicked curveball. What if one of them is the real Silas?

"I'm not going to hurt you," one of the Silases speaks up.

I shift my attention to the sound of the voice, studying the face with caution. This can't be the real one, can it?

"Come here, I will protect you," another Silas says.

Silas would never say that. Not giving it another chance to deceive me, I slam a bolt of energy through it, eyeing it dissolving into nothing.

Five left.

I scan the rest of the faces, doing another three-sixty.

"Willow, it's me. The one you're fated to...you have to see it's me."

What a mistake. Silas doesn't talk about *fate* unless I force him into it. He would never so willingly say something like that.

I take another Silas down.

Four remaining.

They all take a hesitant step forward.

*"How will you choose the right one?"*

"Why are you doing this?" I yell into the night.

Sydney glances up from his post, going immediately back to work on sealing the crack.

*"Pick a Silas, Willow...you're wasting everyone's time."*

Pick a Silas? As if my decision doesn't matter. Because none of these are the real Silas.

I close my eyes, breathing deeply, searching and scanning for the man I'm connected to.

I blink back into reality and exhale, spinning in a swift circle, blasting each remaining Silas with the sharpest energy I can summon.

I fall to the ground, not daring to watch what I've done, to verify whether or not I made the right decision.

Tears flow, and my emotions bubble up and take hold. I fold into myself, so fucking afraid for what I've done.

# CHAPTER 19

The world goes quiet. There are no voices, no sounds of the forest, only my ragged and labored breaths.

I have to look, to see what I've done, but I can't bring myself to face the reality of potentially making the wrong decision.

The possibility alone is enough to destroy me.

The image of Silas lying lifeless in the shadow realm consumes me. His body was limp and utterly motionless. His head in my lap. The sheer rage that built and flooded over.

I'm fortunate that my explosion did no harm to Cameron, Deghan, and Sydney.

But regardless, I made the mistake of hurting Silas and putting everyone else in danger.

"Willow," a voice calls out. So fucking recognizable.

I whip my head in its direction, my body lurching backward as yet another Silas comes running forward. My hands strain against the ground, blood flowing from my cuts. I wince and throw my arms up to block whatever is approaching, the tears spilling down. I don't have it in me to defeat another Silas. If this is the end, then so be it. I can't continue to destroy even a fake version of him anymore.

Not concerned with the possibility of me hurting him, he skids to a stop at my feet, immediately tugging me into his arms. The painful touch of the demon never comes, only the blissful embrace of Silas Harlow, the very real one.

I don't mean to, but I flinch.

"It's me. I promise. It's me. It's your Silas. You did it. It's over. Oh, Willow. Are you okay?"

I sob, my arms pressed awkwardly between his and my chest. I shake my head. "How...how are you here?"

"There was a barrier. I couldn't get in. Angels, I tried. I watched the whole thing. I felt everything. I'm so sorry. The moment you destroyed the last one, the wall broke free."

Footsteps sound on the ground, alerting me to an approaching person.

My body tenses, and my Silas holds tighter.

A growl permeates from him. "Get away."

"Is she...is she okay?" Sydney asks.

I push away from Silas, using his shoulder to bring myself up. I point a furious finger at Sydney. "You stay away from me."

Sydney's face drops, and his hands move toward me.

Silas vamp-speeds between us. "You heard her." His shoulders square; he's prepared to stand his ground.

"Willow, I..." Sydney mutters. "You have it all wrong."

"Whatever we had, Sydney, we're done. Do you hear me? Done."

My heart breaks at the declaration, but how can I continue to allow someone in my life who has put me in such danger? The worst part of all is he's hiding something even greater from me that I've yet to figure out.

"I can explain, please." Sydney takes a step.

Silas throws his forearm into Sydney's chest, stopping him from moving.

"Please," Sydney begs.

I shake my head, the fatigue of the battle hitting me, the open wounds on my body throbbing and bleeding everywhere.

Silas shoves Sydney and then swoops me into his arms, rushing us away, into the forest, and leaving Sydney behind.

It's not long until we reach a cabin, tucked between layers of trees.

"Where are we?" The uncertainty of whether I should trust Silas creeps in. How can I be sure of anything anymore? What if Silas has bad intentions, too?

We step across the threshold and into the cozy building. I scan the contents, everything seeming so his style. Dark, moody, but clean and organized.

"I can sense your worry, Willow. And words are words, but I promise you, I mean you no harm." He puts his hand to his chest. "It would kill me to hurt you."

Silas's steel-gray eyes captivate me, and without realizing it, I raise my hand to his face.

I go to speak but catch sight of my bloodied palms. I jerk my arm quickly down to my side, not wanting to throw any natural alarms off in Silas's head.

How he's so capable of controlling his thirst I'll never be able to understand. But maybe what we learn in stories isn't always true.

Silas latches onto my wrist, turning it over and running a finger along the outside of the wound.

"May I?" he asks gently.

I sit on the edge of the king-sized bed and extend my hand.

He kneels on the floor between my legs, gently taking my

offering. He brings his own hand to his mouth, opening wide and allowing his fangs to fully protrude.

They're long and sharp and elegantly magnificent.

Silas bites into his palm, drawing blood like he did the time I hurt myself shaving, and carefully strokes it against my cut. Within seconds, my lesion heals itself, the pain floating away as if it was never there, only the memory of it remains.

He delicately lets go, possessing my other hand and repeating the motion.

Once both are fixed, he focuses his attentiveness to my mangled legs.

My shins, knees, even my thighs are cut and sliced open, skin dangling around the edges of my pants. Dirt and debris cake the layers between blood and fabric and skin.

Sighing and shaking his head, he gets to work.

He starts low, healing what he can seem to reach, moving up and up.

His touch is paradise, and the relief from the restoration is glorious.

He grazes his palm across my mid-thigh, and it's all I can do to sit still. Every so often, his gorgeous eyes meet mine for a look of approval, sending sparks flying in my chest.

His fingers roam to my waist, hooking into my belt loops, tugging the material.

"Are you ever going to tell me what this is between us?" I whisper.

Silas's jaw tightens, one of his most obvious tells. "I can't...it's not fair to you."

"Tell me something, then, please," I beg.

He doesn't meet my eyes, only trails his hand over my legs, covering what he can of my exposed wounds.

I unbutton my jeans, wiggling them over my hips and allowing Silas to finish pulling them the rest of the way off.

His voice is soft when he finally speaks. "I was paralyzed, swimming in a fog of nothing. Going through the motions. I was empty inside. Hollow. I've lived countless years with this pit of a soul, longing for an unknown. There's always been *something* missing. It wasn't until *you* that I knew it was *someone* who had been missing all along. Seeing you, feeling your presence, it was that last missing puzzle piece finally clicking into place. I needed to know you. To be near you. To exist by your side. But with that, I felt the terrible reality of what was stopping that from happening. It's brutal and beautiful all in one. A disaster of a masterpiece I can't quite wrap my head around. I need you, and in the same instance, I have to stay away from you. It kills me and fuels me, and honestly, it's been the biggest contradiction I've ever known."

"Silas...I—" My words are cut short.

He ultimately looks up, the hints of metallic purple flickering in his eyes. He leans in, hands on my face, pushing himself into me, pressing his plump lips into mine.

We fall back onto the bed, and I die a thousand blissfully perfect deaths.

His warm lips gliding over mine, his tongue, trailing my own.

Without thinking, I climb on top of him, straddling his waist, inching him closer, daring him to hold me tighter. I drag my fingers up his neck, into his hair, tugging it gently but firmly.

His strong hands grip my thighs, roaming back until they're gliding their way up under my shirt. His touch is like a fire alarm going off in every cell of my body, and I'm desperate for more.

I kiss him deeper, twirling my tongue around his, begging for an inch more of closeness. Not breaking away, I clasp the front of his jacket, pushing it to the side, doing my best to rip it off.

He works with me, freeing himself and tossing the leather thing on the floor.

I reach my hands down, grasping the hem of his shirt, lifting it up, up, up.

It's then that I break away, settling my eyes on his upper half.

I had no idea he was covered in tattoos. I can focus for only a second, him grabbing my face and dragging me right back down and into him.

Silas's hands weave back under my shirt, and in an instant, my bra and top are lying somewhere on the floor.

He firmly wraps his arm around me, moving so swiftly and placing me under him.

I reel him in with my legs and dig my fingers into his back, our lips interlocked in a fiery passion I'll never get enough of.

He hesitates, resting his forehead on mine. "Are you sure?"

Clutching his face between my hands, I stare him in the eyes. "I've never been so sure of anything in my life."

My heart pounds, in my ears, in every inch of my body.

But the moment he sighs, putting his lips back on mine, everything stops, and the only thing I'm aware of is this, right here, right now.

His mouth, his hands, his body pressed so firmly against mine.

He tastes of sunshine and a cool breeze.

It's all so sensual and euphoric, and never in my wildest dreams would I have imagined my first time to be anything like this.

Silas slows down, taking his time removing the last of our clothes, settling back on top of my eager body.

I'm covered in dirt and dried blood and I'm so fucking certain I look like the biggest hot mess ever, but Silas meets my gaze, whispering, "You're flawless, Willow."

I have no idea what I'm doing or what to expect, but at his admission, I do what my body urges me to and position myself better, allowing him to take the next step.

His warm length slides over my sensitive parts and into location.

I bite down a whimper as he enters, the admission both pain and pleasure.

Silas stops, his gaze wandering my face.

"Keep going," I breathe.

He wavers again, but I drag his face onto mine, mingling our lips and forcing my body to collide carefully with his.

I moan against his mouth, the pleasure taking precedence over the pain.

Time passes, our bodies becoming so fucking in sync with each other.

And for once, I'm not focused on all the wrong in my life, just this temporarily divine moment I want to last forever with him.

# CHAPTER 20

I trace my finger along the ink-stained skin on Silas's chest, swirling it lightly. The delicate petals of a flower, what must be a rose, sit right beside an antique pocket watch. The blacks and grays flow beautifully together. I can't help but wonder what it signifies. His immortality?

The colorless flowers break off and transition to a large, sketched skull, but upon squinting, there are things hidden within the eyes and nose. Faces, numbers, various letters.

His entire front side, arms included, are covered in different shades of darkness, and damn is it sexy.

"That tickles," he murmurs.

I smile. "Vampires are ticklish?"

He shifts toward me, reaching under my arm and wiggling his fingers. "Aren't you?"

Laughing, I shake my head. "Stop!"

Silas pulls away, teasing me by poking his finger like he's going to start again. He grins, and it's such a beautiful sight.

"You're so misunderstood," I confess.

He settles back onto his pillow, extending his arm and inviting me in. "I don't mind."

We go silent for a while, and I take the opportunity to replay the last few hours in my mind. Everything that led to being in this cabin together. Not helping but lingering my thoughts on our bodies melting into one another.

"Penny for your thoughts?" I finally say.

He exhales. "I don't deserve you, and it kills me to realize that at any point you could up and disappear again, and who am I to be upset about that when you were never mine in the first place? It's a strange feeling to be so incredibly vulnerable and not being able to do a damn thing about it."

I sit up, leaning on my elbow to get a better look at his face. "That's what you're afraid of? Me leaving again?"

"That, among other things."

"I never meant to hurt you." The words fall flat, not having nearly the impact I want them to. "That's the one thing I've been trying to avoid. But no matter what I do, I keep messing up."

He tucks a strand of silver hair behind my ear. "This isn't your fault. None of this is."

"I find it difficult to think it's not. Everything that's happened has been because of me. My mom is missing. I've broken the shadow realm. I...I killed you." I avert my eyes.

He tips my chin up with his finger. "I'm right here. You have to forgive yourself for that. You can't get rid of me that easily."

"I'm sorry."

He shifts his still naked body, barely covered with the sheet, and comes closer to face me directly. Inches away, our breath mixes. Silas's hand finds mine, leaving a trail up my arm, my shoulder, my neck, claiming a home along my cheek. Leaning forward, his lips graze my own. "You have nothing to be sorry for."

He kisses me, softly at first, then more intensely.

I rotate my body, positioning Silas on top of me. Wasting no time, I seize the opportunity as soon as I feel he's ready.

He grins into my lips, and I revel in the moment with him, just one more time before we have to figure out what to do next.

Silas moves in a way that tells me he's more certain of what I want and need than I am myself. I can only wish I satisfy him in half the way he does me.

His breath hitches, and he pauses to meet my gaze. I don't dare look away, not wanting to sever the extreme connection between us.

My magic flows into him, his into mine, and a purple-and-pink elegant dance pours out around us.

Almost too soon, we climb the mountain, my pleasure heightening with his. At the last second, he presses his lips to mine, and we come crashing down together. Somehow, it's more powerful than the last, and I'm not sure if I'll ever get enough of this.

Our bodies, still locked together, fall into each other. He wraps me into his arms, so tight.

Once my breathing slows down, the safety of his embrace is enough to lull me to sleep.

---

"Your clothes are destroyed," Silas calls out from across the cabin. He stands in front of a tall dark dresser, rummaging through the contents. One by one, he tosses me a few articles. "Those might fit."

Still naked and cross-legged under the covers, I latch onto the sweatpants and T-shirt he threw me. "Is this your house?"

He lets out a laugh. "No, not exactly. A place I can keep some of my things...outside of the school."

"That's nice." I bring the top up to my nose, inhaling deeply.

"This smells of you," I mumble into the fabric. I hold it out in front of me and look it over. Deep gray, almost black, and super plain. "It's perfect." I throw it on and stand on the bed, walking to the edge.

Silas speeds over, his hands landing on my waist. "Allow me."

I wrap my arms around him, and he tenderly deposits me on the floor.

I kiss him in thanks, and the moment I do, desire fills my body again.

His hands grip my body, telling me a story that he feels it, too.

The cold air hits my bare bottom, reminding me of the pants I'm lacking.

Reading my mind, he blindly reaches and secures the joggers. He breaks our connection and gets down on one knee, holding the legs open for me to step into.

I place my hand on his shoulder for stability. "I can get dressed myself."

"I'm happy to help." He slides my foot into the other side, then strokes my skin on his way up, tying the waistband at the top to keep them secure.

How is it possible that him putting my clothes *on* can arouse me so damn much?

"Do you want to tell me what happened with Sydney?" Silas asks.

And like that, the mood is gone.

I sit back on the bed, Silas now putting a pair of his socks on my feet.

"He told me his family had an object that could help me find my mom. Um...a...what the hell was it called?"

"A reperio stone?"

"Yeah! Wait, how did you know what it's called?" I eye him suspiciously.

"The last of the reperio was mined hundreds of years ago, and it's nearly impossible to come by, especially a stone that actually has powers. Only certain witches can bring one to life. I'm not at all surprised they have one." He finishes putting on my dirty shoes and claims a spot next to me on the bed.

"Sydney said his parents had a lot of magical stuff."

"I don't doubt that."

"But how? Why do they need it all?"

"They're thieves, Willow." His face tenses. "You didn't tell him...about your angel blood, did you?"

I shake my head. "No, I swear."

He sighs. "Good. You have to be careful who you trust."

I flip a loose strand of string between my fingers, avoiding his eyes. "And why should I trust you?"

"Don't. Please. Don't. Be cautious with everyone." He places his hand on top of mine. "But never in a million years will I do you wrong. That I promise you."

I process his statement, the energy coursing through the room. Something deep inside me accepts, believes him fully without reservations.

"What are we going to do?" My belly grumbles, telling me it's time for breakfast.

Silas jumps from the bed, appearing by the refrigerator in a flash. "Pancakes or waffles?"

"You can cook?" I tease.

"When you've been around as long as I have, you have to learn a few skills to survive."

I don't think he means to, but a heavy sadness fills his voice.

I come up behind him, leaning my head on his shoulder. "Waffles."

---

Cleaning off the table post breakfast, I mentally try to form a plan. "We could get the stone," I suggest.

"From their *house*? No way, too dangerous."

"Maybe it's not in their house. Would you recognize it? Sydney went in to get it, and if he was successful, he may have brought it back to the place he's staying. His house is totally separate from the main building and doesn't have the same security." I try to sound convincing.

"We can't risk going out on their property again. Not taking into account what happened." Silas puts on a pair of dark jeans and plucks his jacket from the floor.

"It's stupid hot outside, how can you wear that?"

"I'm a vampire. I can regulate temperature well. Plus, I don't allow people to see my tattoos." He shoves his arms into the sleeves.

"You let me see them..." I grin at him.

"You're the *only* exception." He smiles back. "But we're not getting the stone. Sorry. Not putting you in danger like that. Maybe if we had reinforcements, but no way in hell Walker is going to let us stroll in, get Deghan, and anyone else willing to help. Which would probably be slim to none if we actually tell them what we're after."

"What do you mean?"

"The stone is powerful, but it's dangerous, too. To find the person you're looking for, you have to give it a little piece of you. A blood sacrifice that ties you to it. I've heard stories of people coming into contact with one of those and there being bad reactions."

Sydney never told me that using the stone was hazardous. He only said that it would help me find my mom. He abused my vulnerability and nearly killed me with his foolishness. How could I have been so naïve in leaving the school with him? "I had no idea."

"We need to get you to the school. Walker has it incredibly secure—you're safe there. Protected until we can figure out what to do next."

"Protect me from what, though? The voice is gone, I killed endless demonic versions of you and Sydney..." My mind processes what my mouth won't say.

"Exactly, Sydney could reopen that crack to the demon realm. He can't be trusted."

"Okay." I sigh, not wanting to be a prisoner again, but not wanting to be so fucking vulnerable out here in the open. "Are you sure we can't stay here forever?" I glance over my shoulder at the bed.

"Although that sounds like my kind of paradise, I have to do what's best for you. You're safe here, but only temporarily. My protections won't last much longer."

His protections? It's a strange thing to wrap my head around the fact that vampires have abilities, too.

"Deghan and Cameron must be worried sick," I admit, guilt consuming me at leaving them again.

"I told Deghan I was going to find you. Don't worry, they'll be okay."

We walk outside, the warm morning breeze flowing through the trees.

"How far away are we?"

"At your pace or mine?" Silas holds out his arms. "Hop in."

I shake my head, gripping his shoulder to brace for him picking me up. I wrap my arms around his neck. At least it's an excuse to be this much closer to him.

"Hold on," he says, taking off in a sprint.

A minute goes by of trees whipping past. I breathe in the fading summer air, making way for fall's richness. We appear near the edge of the clearing.

"We're going to have to go in the front, otherwise it'll freak everyone out thinking the school is under attack."

"Walker is going to be so pissed." I hate that I was so reckless in leaving the way I did.

"He's reasonable." Silas places his hand on the small of my back, nudging me forward. "You haven't had any other voices in your head?"

"No." I speak the truth, but something tells me they're not gone for good. There's this weird cloud still hanging around in my mind, this fullness pressing of someone else being in there, too. It has me on alert, waiting for it to appear. Considering Silas has such a powerful connection to me, it'll probably surface when he's not by my side. I have to be prepared if that happens.

"What aren't you telling me?" He can read me like an open book.

Without skipping a beat, I blurt out, "I hate disappointing people."

Silas studies my face, clearly trying to determine whether or not to accept my response.

We approach the gravel entryway to the school, and an abnormal glow surrounds the premises. I follow it up and over the back side—it resembles a glittering dome.

"Protective barrier," Silas answers my unspoken question.

I allow my gaze to lower, settling on Abigail in the distance.

She runs toward us, stopping right at the barricade. "Where the hell have you been?"

# CHAPTER 21

Abigail allows us entry to the grounds, but not without thoroughly scanning us with her hands and then a large wand to make sure we're not possessing a demonic being.

"Is that thing still in your head?" she asks.

I shrug. "I don't think so."

"At least there's *that* silver lining." She leads us toward the building. "Walker is going to want to have a word with you. He's already spoken to Sydney."

Sydney? He's back? He's here, in this building? My skin crawls, and my body gravitates toward Silas.

"He said you two left and he tried to get you to come back," Abigail says with questioning brows.

At the lie, my gaze shoots to Silas.

We continue the rest of the way to the headmaster's office with an awkward silence hanging in the balance. The door clicks shut behind us.

"I see you've decided to rejoin us." Walker shuffles the papers on his desk and then leans back, crossing his arms over his chest. "Care to explain yourselves?"

Silas clears his throat. "We thought that Willow might be able to locate one of her father's possessions, to make the search for her mother easier. It's been greatly bothering her. We should have asked. It's my fault for insisting. If there are any punishments, I ask to accept them solely." Silas stands firmly to my right, his hands to his sides. He doesn't look my way despite me rubber-necking at him.

"And were you successful?" Walker questions, his tone lightening up.

"No, sir," Silas verifies.

"I see. Well, we're all adults here. There will be no penalties, but I do encourage you to inform us if you leave the premises again, although I highly advise against it in the meantime. When you decided to attend this school, you put yourself in my care, and to endanger yourselves and weaken the barrier without a second thought is truly disheartening. I don't want to have to reconsider your admission here." His last few words are the most impactful of all.

"I'm sorry," I finally speak.

"I understand these are troubling times for you, Willow. You have more on your plate than most others. I do hope that you're thoughtful of your actions, though." He stands, walking around his desk and leaning alongside it like he often does.

"If you don't mind, I need to take a break from the shadow realm for the time being. I've been feeling poorly lately and was hoping to rest up and come back stronger." But really, I can't imagine being forced to sit so intimately with the one who deceived me and be required to allow him into my head. My stomach turns knowing how defenseless and exposed I've been to him all this time.

Walker nods. "I had a hunch this would happen. I absolutely understand. Take some time. Recover. We'll pick back up where we left off, but not until you're ready. In the interim, Sydney can provide his power."

They're going to continue without me? Using Sydney? What if Sydney is making the shadow realm susceptible to more demon attacks?

"Good idea," Silas answers.

"Thanks for checking in. Please be more transparent if you plan on departing again."

Silas and I exit the office, my gaze trailing the floor, me trying to process what just went down.

Out of nowhere, a figure comes barreling into me, lifting me off the floor. "You have *got* to stop disappearing like that, Willow."

*Deghan.*

"You're cutting off the circulation in my arms," I spit out under his hold. "I missed you, too."

Cameron pokes his head out from behind Deghan. He waves. "Hi."

"Cam." I reach one of my arms free and pull him in, smooshing him between us.

"Listen, I'm really happy for your little reunion, but we need to go somewhere private." Silas points at Cameron. "Your room."

Cameron wrinkles his brows. "Did you just *speak* to me?"

Silas rolls his eyes. "Yes or no?"

Shaking his head, Cameron waves us on. "Mi casa es su casa."

"Don't you have roommates?" I add.

"Yeah, I'll tell them we need a minute. Is everything okay?" He glances back and examines me from head to toe. "Is that...blood on your shoes?" His voice quiets down to a whisper at the last few words.

Instead of responding, I make my way up the stairs behind

Cameron. Deghan and Silas follow up the rear. Their presence surrounding me helps ease the concern of Sydney being in the same place.

I can't believe I cared for him...that I had feelings for him...that I kissed him.

I step inside Cameron's room, and my sights settle on Lillian, sitting across from Ethan on what I assume is his bed.

The smile leaves her face, and it kills me that I have that effect on her.

Cameron rubs his neck. "Um, sorry. Do you think we could borrow the room for five minutes? I swear I'll make it up to you. I'll give you an hour tonight."

"Make it dealer's choice, and you have an agreement," Ethan demands.

"Whenever."

Ethan stands, and Lillian lets out an exasperated breath, trailing him out of the room.

Cameron latches the door shut, turning toward us and waiting for some kind of answers.

I focus on Silas, willing him to explain.

He relaxes his weight onto the wall beside him. "We have reason to believe Sydney is part of the problem. He took Willow off campus, led her directly into a trap that nearly cost her life. He's back on school grounds, and I'm not sure what he's planning, but he can't be trusted."

"Holy shit," Deghan blurts out. "You're serious?" He concentrates on me. "Are you okay? Did he hurt you?"

"No, I'm okay. But Silas is very serious. He tricked me into thinking he would help me find my mother."

"He came back in a rush. We tried to talk to him, but he kept throwing up his arms and telling us to get away." Cameron sits on the bed closest to the door.

"Deghan," Silas speaks. "You and I will rotate shifts." He glances at Cameron. "No offense."

Cameron nods. "Yeah, I get it."

Deghan shoots Cam a sympathetic look.

"You good to start now?" Silas asks Deghan.

I shift my attention to him, a strange fear consuming me. "Where are you going?"

"Sydney."

"What? No. He's *dangerous*, you've said it yourself," I insist.

"If anyone should confront him it should be me." Silas kicks off the wall, standing back on both feet. "I won't be long."

The last time I heard that, Sydney left me behind in his house, only to lead me into a deadly trap. I stand there, jaw basically dropped, watching Silas walk out the door, a piece of me leaving with him.

"It'll be okay, little one," Deghan confirms.

"Can we run to the girls' dorms? I want to try to talk to Lillian, if that's okay." I can't continue to allow this fracture to tear us apart. I need my friend in my life. Almost dying kinda puts the important things into perspective, and Lills is one of those very things.

"Hmm...I suppose. It's farther away from Sydney's room so it should be okay. But we're doing a sweep of the dorm first and staying put right outside the door."

"Okay."

I'd agree to any of his terms to get a chance with her.

We exit Cam's space—Cameron in front, me in the middle, and Deghan in the rear. When we get to the end of the hall, Deghan comes around to the front, scanning the open upstairs sitting area, then waving us on.

His eyes glow a golden hue, his wolf instincts activated.

Arriving at my old dorm, I knock on the door.

Kyra answers, beaming at the sight of me. "'Bout damn time!"

"Hey, lady. I was wondering if Lillian was here and if I could talk to her...alone." I bite at the inside of my lip.

"Yes, of course." Kyra opens the door wide, allowing me to enter. She settles her gaze on my entourage. She strolls to her bed, grabbing her purse. "Sorry, Lill, you two need this."

Deghan casually glides in, being totally chill about his inspection of the room.

"I like what you've done with the place," he adds.

Kyra gives him a gentle push toward the door. "Scram."

They funnel out, Deghan glancing over his shoulder to wink at me on his way.

I summon my courage, trying to find the words I need.

Lillian clears her throat, signaling me to get the hell on with it.

"Listen." I pace in front of her bed. "I'll never be able to tell you enough how sorry I am for disappearing the way I did. The dorm change came at a really weird time, and I sort of shut down and needed to be alone. Some *things* are going on that are new and overwhelming, and I'm sorry that I had to leave you in the dark the way I did." I take a breath, unsure of how my apology came across.

"I'm not stupid, Willow, you're hiding something from me. And maybe it's none of my business, but it's really hard not to feel like it is. Your explanation seems...off. I want to forgive you, I really do, but I'm struggling with it." She crosses and uncrosses her hands on her lap.

"You're right, Lillian. There are bits and pieces that I'm not telling you, but it's not because I don't *want* to, it's because I *can't*. Please trust me on this. I'm so sorry I hurt you, and if it takes me a million years to make it up to you, I will, but please let me try."

"I don't expect you to tell me everything that's going on in your life, but you realize how *strange* you're being? We went from being super close to you literally vanishing." She locks her gaze with mine. "I don't let many people in, so this is that much harder on me. I'm pretty damn accepting and the least judgmental...I wish you would have told me you needed some time. Because from my end, all that came across was that you didn't care. About me. About Remi and Kyra. About anyone other than yourself. I get that we haven't known each other long but I consider you one of my best friends."

"You're right, and absolutely justified in feeling that way. I promise you it was never my intention to hurt you. If anything, it was the opposite. Trust me, I don't let people in easily either. There wasn't a day that went by I didn't regret what I did. But I'm not lying when I say I *truly* thought what I was doing was for the best, even if it seems to be the opposite." I sit on the bed next to her.

She finally cracks a smile. "Fine, but I'm not letting you off easy."

My eyes light up. "What? Really?"

Lillian leans in for a hug. "I really did miss you, you little shit."

"Uh, you have no idea how good it is to hear you say that. I thought you hated my guts."

"No, not unless you kick a puppy or something."

I gasp dramatically. "I would never—I love puppies."

"Right? Who doesn't love puppies?"

Remi walks in, beaming at the sight of us. "Awe, you two finally made up."

I grip onto a pillow and chuck it at her.

She tries to dodge it, but it smacks her in the face. "Rude!" She laughs. "What are you wearing?"

I glance down, Silas's oversized T-shirt and sweatpants still hanging on my body.

"And gross, what's up with your shoes?"

"Judgy much? It's been a rough twenty-four hours."

"You girls good?" Deghan pops his head into the room, scanning for anything different than his first examination.

I shift my gaze to Lillian.

She nods slightly. "Yep."

A weight lifts from my shoulders, and somehow, despite every damn thing that keeps going wrong, I feel one step closer to happiness.

"Great, because we need to get moving." Deghan opens the door.

Squeezing Lills's hand, I say, "We have a lot of catching up to do soon, okay?"

"I'd say so." She whips her head toward the door.

I exit the room a renewed woman, ready to take on the world. "Can we *please* go to my dorm now? I'm in desperate need of a shower."

Cameron leads the way, turning down the west wing hallway.

My dorm room door swings open, and we collectively go rigid.

Deghan gravitates in front of me, his body tensing in response.

Ruby appears, hands in the air. "It's just me. Silas asked me to do a sweep of your room."

I examine her energy, determining she's telling the truth. I reach out to Deghan and shove my calming powers into him. "She's okay."

A slight shiver runs over him. "You sure?"

"Positive." I step around him. "Thank you, Ruby."

"Sorry, Rubes." Deghan punches her shoulder as she walks by him. "Things are a little crazy around here."

"I'd say so. You know me better than that, though, shame on you." She hits him back, harder than his blow. "I'm across the hall if you need me."

---

Stepping under the hot water, I close my eyes, allowing the downpour to rinse me from head to toe. I open them and catch sight of the dirty shower floor. I kick my foot around, doing my best to direct the grossness down the drain.

Between this and the fooling around, Silas is going to have to wash those sheets of his.

I rejoice in the memory, our bodies tangled together in a heap of passion and endless desire. If things were different, I would have stayed there forever with him.

But that's not what the world has in store, and it would have only been so long until I longed for the other missing pieces of this messed-up puzzle—Deghan and Cam. Why does it seem so wrong to still want Sydney, too?

I'll never understand what I did to justify having such men in my life, each one of them bringing me more happiness than they'll ever understand.

But what do I give them?

I'm a constant disappointment, hurting them despite my efforts not to.

It doesn't take a voice in my head to tell me they deserve better.

"You okay?" Deghan hollers through the bathroom door.

"Yep." I shut off the water, wringing out my hair, drawing back the curtain only to realize I don't have a towel. "Deghan," I call out.

Loud thuds hit the floor when he runs back. "What's wrong?"

I giggle. "Nothing. I forgot my towel. Can you grab one? They should be on the bed closest to you."

The door cracks, and steam pours out of the room. A towel is extended, attached to his cinnamon-colored arm. His other hand is covering his eyes, and I can't help but laugh again watching him blindly walk into the wall.

"Follow the sound of my voice..." I drag out my words dramatically.

He gets close enough that I can reach and wrap the towel around my still wet body.

"You can look now," I consent.

He peeks through two fingers, then removes his hand. "Damn."

I grin, stepping out of the shower and wiping the mirror off to take a better look.

"You're stupid good-looking."

"Did you hit your head while I was gone?" I stretch my hand out and cup his face.

He sighs. "Nope."

We stare into each other's eyes, the mood shifting from light to more serious.

He glances down to my lips, and the second he moves forward, the door to my dorm opens, startling us both.

Silas saunters by the bathroom, stopping and doing a double-take, a sheet of folded paper held out in his hand.

"It's from Sydney."

# CHAPTER 22

"It's all a lie, right?" The note is held tightly in my grip. My heart pounds, but what if it's not a lie, what if he's telling the truth?

Silas furiously shakes his head. "Maybe. It could be. But at this point, I hate to say that I'm not sure. As much as I dislike him, anything is possible."

"Let me see." Deghan takes the letter from my hand.

Cameron hovers next to him, giving them both the ability to read it.

I tuck my towel tighter around me, realizing I'm still super naked over here.

"He definitely took a sleeping potion. He's out cold. He's alive, breathing, but he's not waking up anytime soon." Silas walks over to my dresser, sliding a drawer open.

"He drugged himself to prove to you he's not trying to hurt you? That's intense, Wills. Don't get me wrong, Sydney is odd and all, but I never once doubted that the dude cared about you." Deghan hands the paper to Cam to let him finish reading it.

With a handful of clothes, Silas advances to the bathroom, going inside and then coming out empty-handed. "Get dressed."

I do what he says, dressing in the clothes that he picked out. With an exhale, a sense of rejuvenation fills me with the fresh wardrobe. I come out barefoot, going to the basket of clean laundry to find a pair of socks.

As I sit on the bed, Silas comes over and takes the socks from me and puts them on my feet himself. His constant need to take care of me is a bit overkill but sweet, nonetheless.

"We should tell Abigail and Walker, right? I mean, if he's telling the truth, what if he's in danger?" I lift my right leg up, sitting on it, getting more comfortable. If Sydney really *isn't* trying to cause me harm, then what the fuck happened back at his house? He *did* seal the crack back up, disallowing the demons from respawning. But it was *his* property, his parents' property.

It finally dawns on me. His parents.

The mom and dad he's constantly disagreeing with and never seeing eye to eye. The ones who were always so formal and hard on him. What if it wasn't Sydney but them who lured us there and summoned the demon? What if it's been them all along?

I detach myself from my thoughts, missing half of whatever Silas had said.

"What do you know about Sydney's folks?" I cut him off.

"Um, they're LeBlancs, and I've already told you what I think of them. Why?"

I shake my head. "It wasn't Sydney, it never was. Did you see the way his mom gawked at me on family day? I'd bet all the magic in the world it was her this whole time."

"We'll have to wake him up and ask him ourselves."

We're through the west wing in a flash, crossing into Sydney's room. My gaze falls on his motionless body lying on his bed. He doesn't appear as peaceful as one would seem if they were sleeping. His face is tense, almost like he's in pain.

I'm at his side in a second, studying him all over. I spot a glass on the nightstand next to him. I pick it up, examining it, smelling the dark-purplish remains.

"Blueberry?" I hold it out to the guys.

Deghan takes a whiff. "Definitely blubes."

I rack my brain trying to think of what kind of potion he could have possibly made. I lay my palms on his chest, closing my eyes and absorbing what I can. The aching energy is vaguely familiar.

I glance around the room. "Hand me that big clear crystal." I point to the stand near his desk where other various crystals are strewn about.

Cam secures it, giving it to me to place on Sydney's chest.

Not having any idea what I'm doing, I breathe deeply, willing my mind to clear. I reverse the flow of my powers, preparing to pull them out, not push them in. A jolt of throbbing energy flows into my hands, up my arms, and into my core. It's heavy and threatens to weigh me down.

"Willow," Silas speaks up, interrupting my concentration. "You need to be careful."

I'd wager to say he can feel exactly what I'm feeling, the unknown negative power tapping into me.

I block him out, siphoning the darkness from Sydney, taking it into my body to deal with itself.

Sydney stirs, confirming my suspicions were correct. It wasn't a sleeping potion, he consumed his glitch—enough of it to render him completely defenseless. Sydney's glitch is blueberries.

He sits up in a rush, taking a gigantic breath of air into his lungs. "You're here," he mutters with the saddest eyes.

"I'm here." I pause only slightly. "I need you to tell me what happened. I need the truth." The concern of his condition is being put on the backburner while I search for the missing information.

He meets my eyes. "My mom...she told me about the stone at family day. She planted the seed, and it's continued to eat me alive since then, knowing we had something to help you find your mom. I had no idea she wanted me to act on it. She urged against it...told me she wasn't willing to help, that we don't do charity cases. I had no idea she was manipulating me to lure you out there. Willow...I'm so sorry. I never meant for you to come into any danger. I swear it on my life."

His energy is pure, straightforward.

"Who is she working for?" Silas chimes in.

Sydney glances up at him and shrugs. "They don't tell me that kind of stuff. They're very private." He focuses back on me. "I never would have taken you there if I knew what they were planning." Sydney grabs onto my hand, his magic flowing into mine.

His voice drifts into my head. *"Please forgive me."* His eyes betray a desperate longing.

*"I need some time."* I withdraw my hand.

Sydney swallows and nods. "Okay."

"If you ever pull a stunt like that again, I will rip you in two," Silas growls. "You may have lucked out this time, but if so much as a hair on her head is hurt on your behalf, you'll have wished—"

I hush Silas, placing my hands on his chest and forcing him to calm down. "He's not going to hurt me. He didn't know. We all make mistakes." It takes more effort than normal to calm him, the glitch still being processed in my system.

How can I struggle to absolve Sydney if I'm guilty of making wrong decisions in the past, too?

"Did you find the stone?" I ask Sydney.

He rises from the bed, walking over to his backpack. Syd reaches inside, bringing out a deep-crimson rock. It sparkles in the light.

"No, absolutely not," Silas interrupts.

"They have risks, Willow. I didn't tell you that before because I knew how badly you wanted to find your mom. But you need to be aware that using the stone can be dangerous." Sydney sighs.

"That's why I thought that we could destroy it once we've found her."

"Wait, what?" I glance from the stone to his radiant green eyes.

"Whatever power you give it will be demolished along with it, eliminating any threat it may pose." He flips it over in his hand.

"Aren't those things super hard to come by, really rare?" I add.

"It's nothing compared to you."

"But..."

"No, I've already decided. You need to find your mom, and I refuse to put you at risk. This is the only way. I'll do anything to prove to you that you're worth more than some magical rock or family ties."

"Family is important to our kind," he had said to me during our intimate shadow realm repair sessions.

He holds the stone out to Silas. "Here, she trusts you, so you can have this for safekeeping."

How can it be possible that Sydney is sacrificing so much right now? This important magical thing, his relationship with his blood relatives, his defiant distaste with vampires. He's doing all of this for me? All when I accused him of scheming behind my back. I got in his face and told him that what we had was over. I demanded that he stay away. I can't imagine how that felt, knowing what I do now.

I thought I was a fool for believing him then, but I was really just an idiot for doubting him. We all have our secrets, but his intentions were never to do the things I had thought he was capable of.

"We'll think about it." Silas takes the stone into his hand, eyeing it with great scrutiny.

"Doesn't seem like a terrible idea." Deghan sits on the bed across from me.

"I would focus on getting rid of that thing in your head first. It weakens you. So it may weaken the connection you have to your mother," Sydney says.

How can I do something I have no idea how to? "I would if I could. It's not that easy. I've tried to no avail. It's latched on in some permanent way, and I can't break its hold."

"Keep trying. You'll figure it out. You're strong, stronger than you think."

Back inside my dorm, Cameron and Deghan decide they're going to go together to get lunch and bring it to us. They both hug me and go on their way.

I turn around, and Silas stands a few feet away.

He extends his arms, and I walk on over to him.

"What are we going to do?" I mumble into his chest.

Tugging my face, he clutches it in his hands. Silas presses his warm lips to mine for a long moment. "We've got to free your mind."

I shake my head. "It's impossible."

"No, it isn't. Nothing is impossible." His eyes pulse with their violet hue. "Do you remember not too long ago...doing this..." He grazes his hand along my cheek. "Was unbearable? *You* made it happen. You did. Now, nothing can stop us from touching. You made the unimaginable come to life."

"I knew what it took to break the curse, though. And I killed you, Silas." The defeat of not knowing how to fix this is growing wild.

"You have to think. You can figure this out." He tilts up my chin. "I believe in you. More than any other force on the planet."

An idea strikes, but I push it away, not wanting to give any clues to the demon possessing my mind. "Do you think you could give me some time alone?" I lean up and whisper in his ear, "Trust me."

# CHAPTER 23

I spell the door shut, then mosey on over to my bed, the absence of Silas filling my body. Lying back, I note the haze creeping in, just as I had expected.

*"Hello, old friend,"* I think.

*"I'm no fool to your tricks,"* it responds.

*"I thought maybe we could chat for once...I could learn about the person invading my mind."* I speak in a cool, calm, and collected manner.

*"I am no person, nor one sole entity. I am all things combined into a host."*

*"That's interesting. Do you have a body?"*

*"Of course, I have a body, you imbecile."*

*"Oh, how was I supposed to know?"* I hesitate. *"Could you show me?"*

*"Why, aren't you a curious one..."*

*"You could say that. If your plan succeeds, which I see no reason for it not to, why not grant me this one thing?"*

*"Ahh, you've finally given up?"*

*"Unless you want to confess how to get you out of my head, then no. It's been weeks, and I've made no progress."* I sigh in defeat. *"If I stop resisting, can you assure me that no harm will come to my friends?"*

Evil laughter ensues. *"And now you're making demands."*

*"Did you expect anything less?"*

A huff. *"I have no qualms with your associates. Although, that witch will have problems of his own to face soon enough."*

*"What kind of problems?"* My heart speeds up, and I urge it to calm down.

*"You ask too many questions, peasant. Haven't you had your fill?"*

*"You never denied that I could see your form."* I swallow deeply, preparing myself for what's to come.

With my eyes still closed, clouds roll in my line of sight, whipping about and settling. A shape appears and comes forward.

The red emerges first, gloriously tattered crimson wings, attached to a muscular and armored body. The armor shines despite the lack of light in my head. The creature's eyes are solid onyx balls, its lips painted black, contrasting against the fire-red skin. Swirls of darkness cover its arms, almost like tattoos...or blood running through its veins. It clutches a long wand in its hand, with sharp silver daggers on both ends.

*"Are you satisfied?"* The voice is different now, not the same as mine, but deep and raspy, more suitable to the image I land my sights upon.

Without allowing the demon to retreat, I do the thing I came here to do. Willing it to happen, I summon myself inward, ripping my being from my body and placing it into my mind. The shift is intense, and the change takes longer than I had hoped, but once it does, I glance down, studying the hands attached to the body I brought to life inside my own head.

*"Impossible,"* the demon shouts.

*"Nothing is impossible, you should be aware of that."* I move my hands, getting used to the different atmosphere here. I surge my power forward, and it ripples down my arm and into my hand with a force greater than I've ever known. I must be stronger inside my own head.

The demon turns, looking for a way out, but I disallow it, kneeling and then throwing a blast of energy into the space, creating a dome blocking his exit.

*"Now, now,"* I taunt. *"Leaving so soon?"*

*"You want a battle? I'll give you one."* It thrusts the shaft into the ground, hurling a burst of energy through it.

I stumble but regain my footing in a flash, twirling my hands around and throwing a ball of power its way.

The demon dodges it and stalks forward.

*"I need a weapon,"* I whisper to myself. The air around me whooshes, and a sword appears in my hand, brandished with deep-purple highlights.

Purple? My magic is pink.

I turn it over. A green glow radiates from the other side, and the handle sparkles of gold.

*The guys.* They've somehow given me some of their power. How that's even possible, I don't have the luxury of time to figure out right now.

The weapon is perfectly my size, not too big, not too small, the appropriate weight to fit into my hand with ease, becoming an extension of myself.

I wave it to and fro in an attempt to get acquainted with it, and it glitters with power, leaving trails of misted magic in its wake.

*"Are you done playing games?"* The demon steps sideways like he's stalking his prey.

At least I think it's a *he*. The masculine build and manly bravado could be misleading.

Instead of letting him lead, I take a cautious yet confident leap toward him, sending him unsure of where to move next.

Once I'm close enough, I spin around, slashing at him with my sword, deflecting when he blocks my blow and defends himself.

*"This will be a rather enjoyable experience."* He slams his weapon into mine, the blades clanking loudly and sparking with a mix of colors. *"You cannot defeat me."* Another blow, this time low.

I jump, missing the attack, and once I'm midair, I swing, slicing a bare section of his upper arm. A vivid emerald dazzles from the blade.

*Thanks, Sydney.*

*"Luck,"* the demon spits. *"You have no talent, no skill. The only reason you've made it thus far is pure luck."*

I take off in a sprint, circling the demon, running up the dome shielding behind him, and swinging my sword across his exposed back. *"You call that luck?"* Golden flickers in the dimness of the area.

*Deghan.*

*"You will never make it out of here alive. Your friends will not mourn you; they will move on and live better lives without you pathetically dragging them down."*

*"Is that so?"*

*"Nothing. You are nothing, Willow Oliver."* He lunges forward, an undiluted rage boiling from him. The sword, gripped in both of his hands, comes flying down onto me.

I kneel and raise my weapon. It seems measly compared to his, but the punch it packs is lethal. I shield my face, not sure whether it will withstand the blow, but somehow it sends the demon staggering back the moment the two come into contact. Violet sparks go everywhere, raining down around me.

*Silas.*

I take the opportunity to stand, firm on both feet. *"You're wrong."* I pursue him. *"You don't know a damn thing about me."*

The demon glances out of the corner of his eye, clearly trying to locate a way out while I back him into the wall.

*"I can sense your fear,"* I say. *"You are damn well aware that you are outmatched."*

At this, the demon huffs, throwing down his weapon. It vaporizes, and for the slightest second, I think I've won, that he will submit and plead for my mercy to be set free.

But I was wrong.

And instead, multiple small daggers appear in both of his hands, and a devilish grin spreads across his evil face. Without me being able to react, he throws one toward me, and it lands deeply in my left thigh. Pain, blisteringly hot and nothing I've ever experienced before, rattles through me. He throws another. This one finds a home inches away from the first. The third grazes my thigh and wedges into my pants.

I bite down a terrified scream, not wanting to allow him the satisfaction of his upper hand.

My vision goes white, and the only thing I can think to do is reach down, gripping the serrated blades impaled in my thigh and rip them out.

*"Shall I say I told you so?"* The demon sneers.

I infuse the bloodied knives with my magic and send one flying as soon as my sights come back, totally catching him off guard.

The metal penetrates his leg, in the same spot he had hit me. He heaves forward, true pain surging into him, and damn is it a glorious sight.

*"You...you..."* He stutters and slurs his speech, incapable of forming words through the agony. *"Your blood."*

My blood? What about it? Is that what doubled him over? I glance at my leg, unsure of what the fuck he's talking about. I shift my focus at something in my peripheral—a faint glowing of white wings flashes and then disappears.

*Angel blood.*

I hold the soaked weapon tightly in my hand, scraping against my gushing wound, making sure to cover it fully. I throw it with such force that it slices through his armor and impales his shoulder.

He falls onto his hind side, flopping about like a fool. Terror and such shock consume his features.

*"Bitch!"* he screams. *"There is no help for you. Regardless of what happens here, you will never win. This life you think you own is not yours, as you are a puppet in something much bigger. Forever you will be bound to serve another."*

*"You're wrong. You are another pathetic lackey that I will take down on this quest to free my people. Whatever you think they have in store for me, I will be prepared to take on each challenge when they come."* Ripping the last dagger from my bottoms, I drag my injured leg and limp toward him, determination superseding the anguish.

I swipe it across my hand, pooling fresh blood from the self-made wound, wiping it back and forth across the blade. Standing atop the weakened demon, watching him grapple at his own daggers lodged into his body, I wave my hand over his form, the hot droplets sizzling on impact.

*"You will be alone forever. No one cares about you, not the way you think they do. You are never going to amount to anything."* His voice is strained, nothing like the arrogant demeanor he once exuded. *"All of the things I've been telling you are no more than what you already fear."*

I shake my head, tears threatening to tumble down, but not sad ones in response to his statement, but because I realize how terribly wrong he is, how stupid I ever was for allowing him to weaken me.

I am an Oliver witch, descended from the angels themselves. I am potent and resilient.

*"Your words, your pointless attempts to take what will never be yours. It's all been for nothing other than making me realize my*

*true strengths,"* I grit out through my teeth, the immense sharp spikes of pain still hitting me. *"You are not real."*

I slam the dagger into his chest cavity, the force rattling through my hands.

His blackened mouth bubbles over with a thick tar-like substance, and the existence leaves his already dead-looking eyes.

The demon explodes, specks of black and red filling the air and dissolving, sending me falling onto the empty ground.

I lie there, turning over and reaching upward, pulling the magic from the dome back into my body. The returning force slams me up and then down, hard.

My head tilts to the side, and I mutter, "Come in," breaking the spell I had put on my room as everything fades to black.

# CHAPTER 24

Sometimes, no matter how hard you try, your efforts never pay off. Failure is this thing you grow accustomed to, almost like an old friend you secretly despise, but accept that they'll be in your life forever. It becomes something you can rely on, something you make a place for regardless of whether it's what you want.

But then sometimes, you realize you have to be more concerned with succeeding, rather than focused on failing. And once you unlock that knowledge, you can do anything if you put your mind to it, because failure will no longer be this thing you fear, but something you can live with and overcome. Something that won't stop you from fulfilling your destiny, but something that tells you you're on the right path. Great things aren't easy, and the biggest rewards come from perseverance.

You only have to hone the will to push forward and make it happen.

At least, that's what I told myself in my last moments.

And when the angels greeted me, magnificent and breathtakingly beautiful, wings spread and hovering in what appeared to be clouds, they rotated their hands, spinning me around and throwing me back to where I came from.

My eyes flip open, and I suck in a staggering breath of air, sitting straight up.

Hands, from all directions, grabbing at my body. Watchful stares, so terrified and relieved, soaking into me.

Deghan, his shaky arms wrapped around my torso, his face pressed against my side.

Cameron, with his pleading and watery eyes, clutching at his chest.

Sydney, panting, so out of breath, his brow furrowed in disbelief, his hands falling, like he was doing some kind of spell.

Silas, complete terror resolving into liberation.

"I'm here." My voice cracks.

"You...you died." Deghan doesn't let go, only holds me tighter.

I meet Silas's gaze, and the shock on his face breaks me. I reach out my hand to him, dragging him down and onto the bed.

Sydney clears his throat. "Your heart, it stopped beating."

"I'm alive." I reach for one hand at a time, laying them on my chest, letting them each feel my beating heart. "See."

"What happened?" Cameron finally asks. "Where did you go?"

"I knew the only way to get rid of the thing in my head was to go in and defeat it myself. I couldn't just will it away, so I had to take a more direct approach. I don't really know how I knew, or how I did it, but I went inside my mind and I battled it." I process the very strange memory. "I needed help, and I asked for it...a sword appeared, brandished with your magic," I nod to Sydney, "and yours," I tap Deghan's shoulder, "and yours," I squeeze Silas's hand.

"I'm sorry I couldn't help," Cameron says with such a sense of sadness.

I shake my head. "You're always with me, right here." I press my hand to my heart.

"I've...Willow, I've never seen anything like that in all my experience of being a witch. I've never so much as heard of what you did." Sydney frantically tries to make sense of the situation. "How did you defeat him?"

I peek at Silas out of the corner of my eye. "I put up a block which stopped allowing him to weaken my defenses. We went back and forth for a while, exchanging blows. He landed a few solid hits." I reach down to my thigh, the phantom ache remaining on my uninjured leg. "And after a fierce battle, I stabbed him through the heart with one of his own daggers. Then I unspelled the door and..." The rest is a mystery, one where apparently, I died and was pushed back to life by the angels. Or maybe that was only a dream.

Deghan moves, staring at me with those golden eyes of his. "The voice is gone now?"

I breathe in, relishing in the total clearness of my mind. "Yeah."

And damn, that's a good revelation, to completely be free of those horrible thoughts. The ones I created, and the demon took advantage of. My innermost vulnerabilities and insecurities, massively dramatized and used against me to weaken my mind and allow that *filth* to get the upper hand. We all have things that worry us, but they should never take such precedence and cripple us from living to our fullest potential. How pathetic that this curse has to go through such lengths to try to steal my magic.

"What do you need?" Cam asks, clearly wanting to be of some assistance. "Are you hungry, thirsty, tired? Name it, and I'll get whatever you want."

"Weren't you making lunch?" How long have I been out?

"Yeah, until you locked yourself in here. Then it pretty much became this chaos of trying to get in. I can go finish, but promise me you won't do that again." His eyes are pleading.

"I promise." And I really mean it.

"You want to come?" Cam pokes Deghan on the shoulder.

Deghan sighs heavily, his arms not wanting to let me free. "Pinky promise?"

I wiggle a hand free, locking my little finger into his. "I'll be right here when you get back."

The two slowly leave the room, and once they're gone, an overwhelming exhaustion hits me full force. I struggle to keep my eyes open despite the sting and end up leaning into Silas's strong body.

"I guess this means you can use the stone whenever you're ready. I didn't anticipate you to act so quickly on uncompromising your mind." Sydney maintains his distance at the foot of the bed.

The fracture between us, not seeming to ease.

"Could we have a moment alone?" Silas speaks up, stiff and firm, dominant.

Sydney nods. "Of course." He moves immediately, not hesitating to exit the room.

"Syd!" I call out.

He stops but doesn't turn around.

"Come back in a few minutes and eat with us. Please."

"It's okay," is all he says. He finishes his exit, taking a part of me with him.

The room grows quiet until Silas speaks.

"You scared the shit out of me. I...I *felt* you die. I could tell the second you slipped away, and in all the deaths I've experienced, none of them compare to that. It was something I can't describe. This venomous pit opening up inside me, seeping into every inch of my body. And there was nothing I could do to stop it. *Nothing*."

"I'm sorry." The one thing I keep finding myself saying to

those I care about. I grip his face in my hands. "I'm here now. I'm safe. Safer than I was hours ago."

His gaze latches on to mine. "I can't live in a world without you."

"You don't have to." I bring my face to his, but he stops me.

"I'm serious, Willow. I won't do it."

The meaning behind his words clicks into place. "Silas..."

"I've lived long enough to be certain that I refuse to do it deprived of you again."

I move, and this time there are no restrictions, my lips landing on his, fighting for their perfect home. I breathe him in, desperate for him to see that I don't want things any other way.

A heated moment passes, and he draws back. "I need you to understand that I'll never make you choose, nor will I ever expect that. It wouldn't be fair to you. I've lived over a hundred years and I've never felt more alive than I do with you. I won't risk losing you over something so meaningless as jealousy. All I care about is that you're happy and you're safe." He tucks a strand of hair behind my ear. "And that you're loved...unconditionally."

My cheeks redden and turn upward. Is he confessing that he loves me? What is this warm and flowy presence simmering up and out of him and into me? The connection we share is intense and only continues to grow stronger with each passing day.

The sturdy dorm door barrels open, and Deghan and Cameron walk in, arms full.

"Oh shit," Deghan blurts out. "We totally interrupted a *moment*." He stops in his tracks, taking a gradual step back in his dramatic fashion like he's pressed rewind.

"Don't you dare leave!" I command. "I'm starving."

He grins from ear to ear and moves forward, approaching the bed with bags of heavenly smelling food.

*Angels.*

"What's wrong? I thought you loved mac and cheese?" Cam startles me from my thought.

I force a smile, but not without Silas catching on to my

weirdness. "Um, I do. Gimme." I seize a fork from the pile on the bed and take the bowl of steaming deliciousness I'm handed.

"And your protein..." Cam sets a pile of chicken tenders on a plate in front of me then goes back to pour some sauce into a tiny bowl. "Try this and tell me what you think."

Still chomping away at the mac, I secure a tender and dip it into the creation. Once my mouth is cleared enough to not be a disgusting pig, I say, "Holy shit, did you make this yourself?"

Deghan smacks Cameron. "See, I told you it was good."

I smother another piece with sauce and hold it up to Silas. "Try this."

He takes the bite straight from my hand, something so seductive about it, especially the way his gaze penetrates mine. What I wouldn't give for a long moment alone with him. But maybe once I've taken a big fucking nap. I'm exhausted, and this food is going to send me into a coma.

The only thing missing is Sydney.

Although I'm wickedly tired, I take a plate, scooping all the fixings on.

Deghan's eyes go wide. "Are you about to out-eat me for a change?"

I laugh. "That would be impossible, you famished wolf." Standing, I tell the guys, "I'll be right back."

All of them tense, I have to remind them that I'm free, the demon is gone, and for now, nothing else has come crashing down on me.

"Five minutes, that's it. Then I come looking for you." Silas wipes at his mouth with a napkin.

Seeing him so willingly staying behind with Cameron and Deghan warms my heart.

I wander down the hallway, walking along the top of the indoor garden, it never fails to amaze me at its beauty. I round the corner and enter the north wing, stopping in front of Sydney's door.

Like he knew I was approaching, the door opens, and he appears on the other side.

"Hey," I mutter.

He glances at the dish in my hands, then up to me. "What's up?"

"I thought if you didn't want to eat with us...I'd at least bring the food to you." And see if you're okay.

"Oh, well, thanks." Sydney stands still.

"Can I come in?"

He nods. "Yeah, sorry." And he steps out of the way, allowing me entry.

"Listen." I set the food on his desk, rotating to face him. "The things I said to you at your house."

Sydney throws up his hands. "No, it's fine. You don't—"

"No, I'm serious. I was confused. I misunderstood the situation, but it never gave me any right to treat you the way that I did." I push a boundary by reaching out and touching his shoulder, unsure of how he will react. "I can't tell you enough how sorry I am."

His opposite hand extends and lands on mine, a calming comfort at him not pushing me away even though he should. "You really don't have to apologize. I recognize how everything came across. I should have been smarter and never let it happen in the first place. If anything, I'm sorry. I will never forgive myself for putting you in danger like that. My parents...they're ruthless. But I'm done with them, okay?"

How can you just be done with the people who brought you into the world?

"What do you mean *done*?"

He chuckles. "I mean, it was either them disowning me or me disowning them. I can't be any part of *that* anymore. I refuse to have ties to them."

"But you said family is everything to witches." My hand still rests between his and his shoulder.

"Some things are more important than that." His red-rimmed eyes glisten.

Maybe this is what the demon meant with his declaration that the witch would have problems soon enough. Maybe his problems will be that he's thrown out of his coven and left all alone. But it doesn't have to be that way. Aside from my mom, I'm a lone witch in need of others, too. There's no reason for Sydney to be pushed to the wayside.

"You don't have to go through this by yourself." I pull him into a hug, sighing at how much I really did miss him.

Life is crazy and totally unpredictable, but one thing has been proven to me time and time again—if people are willing to be there with you and stand by your side for no other reason than caring deeply, you fucking allow them.

# CHAPTER 25

The guys insist I take the rest of the day off, so I do exactly that.

I nap, I eat some more food prepared by Chef Cam, I nap again, until finally, I sleep so long the sun sets and then rises.

I wake feeling like a renewed woman, getting the rest I needed without that stupid voice provoking me time and time again. It had gotten to the point in the last couple weeks where my dreams weren't safe. They were muddied with horrible visions of killing Silas, the girls refusing to forgive me, and the worst of all, finding my mom, but only too late—her lifeless corpse eating away at my soul.

Which brings me to my task for the day.

Figuring out how the hell to use this magical reperio stone to locate my mother.

"We have to do it in a controlled environment," Sydney says. "Meaning...we're going to have to tell Walker what's going on."

"How exactly do you propose we do that? Isn't he going to ask where the stone came from?" And why have we chosen to not acknowledge it until now?

"I thought about telling him that my mom had brought me a bag of crystals to identify on family day. And I've only recently discovered what it was."

"Do you think he'll buy that?" I ask, not feeling totally confident in his cover story.

"Probably not." Sydney scratches his chin. "I could say it was in a box of stuff I packed from my house when I moved in."

"Or we could tell him the truth." I tilt my head and throw my arms up.

"If you're okay with him kicking me out of the school for lying to his face, then by all means, yeah." Silas brings up a good point.

"True. Let's not do that." I lean into him and stare across the room at Sydney, perched on top of one of the spare beds in my room, a steaming cup of coffee in his hands.

"We need as few people as possible, too. Not all of us will be able to come, and I'm assuming Walker is going to want him or Abigail to supervise. So, with you, one of them, and me, we're pushing it." Sydney avoids Silas's glaring stare.

"Nope, no way in hell." Silas tenses.

I place my hand on his thigh, and like he knows what I'm up to, he pushes me away.

He moves abruptly. "You better not put that calming juju into me right now."

I recoil. "Sorry, I thought you could think more clearly without your heightened emotions."

He turns his attention to Sydney. "I'm not leaving her side. She may have forgiven you, but I haven't."

"Fair enough. I don't blame you." Sydney takes a sip of his drink.

Deghan and Cam enter the room, always together, always super cute.

"We come bearing gifts." Cam holds out his hands. "Or food, whatever. Who doesn't love food?" He laughs, and it's no wonder Deghan loves spending his free time with him.

Bringing a small table from the corner, Deghan places it near Cam, then helps him unload the bags of yummy offerings.

"If anything, we won't starve with you around." I wink at Cam, and he winks back.

We all get plates, scooping up scrambled eggs and sausage—pancakes, too. It's warm and decadent and freaking wonderful.

"What did you guys decide?" Deghan shoves a forkful of pancake in his mouth.

"Sydney said I have to limit who comes with...it's a safety thing, because the stone is so unstable." I take a bite of eggs, letting them melt in my mouth. "Uh, this is so good. You have to open up your own place. Seriously. I'm demanding it."

Cam grins. "Okay, okay."

Deghan looks exaggeratedly hurt. "Willow says so and now you're on board? I've been telling you for *months*."

Shrugging, Cameron says, "You eat *everything*, though."

Their banter is entirely precious.

---

Having a full belly and being surrounded by great people really does a number on the immense worrisome nerves that arise when facing the scary unknown.

But only so much.

And each step closer to the random building not too far hidden in the forest behind the school only rattles me that much more.

Abigail leads the way, Sydney at her side. The two of them quietly chatter back and forth.

Silas's hand is gently resting on my lower back, guiding me forward.

We arrive at the location. A small structure, about the size of Silas's cabin, is tucked between rows of trees. It's old but well-kept.

"This is witch territory," Silas whispers in my ear. "Sacred ground. I shouldn't be here."

I scan his face. "I need you."

"I said *shouldn't*, not that I wouldn't," he confirms.

I step inside, and the stale air assaults me.

Sydney draws something from his pocket, lighting it with a match. He catches my watchful gaze and says, "Sage. Should clear up that musky smell. This place usually sits empty for a while."

Abigail walks to a long table adorned with various objects— different-sized cauldrons and goblets, wooden shafts, quarter-sized pressed pentacles, a rather elegant, white-handled knife. She lights a candle, then a few more, setting them around the cluttered space.

Sydney extends his hand to Silas. "The reperio stone, please?"

Silas sighs, digging it out and handing it to him.

"Willow, this is a fairly simple but powerful procedure. All you're going to need to do is prick a finger, focus on the person you're trying to locate, and open yourself to what the stone offers you. It will connect to you and then track the other person. You have to keep a clear head, though. You can do that, right?" Sydney offers me the shiny red rock.

"Yeah."

"Abigail and I are going to stand at opposite ends of you, creating a barrier around the ritual. Silas," he points to him, "you'll need to stay over there."

I follow his line of sight to near the door. I swallow down the strange loneliness that creeps in at their small distances.

Silas reels me in, holding me close, cupping my face in his hands, staring into my eyes. "You're going to do fine. I'm here with you." He kisses my forehead, lingering his lips against my skin for a hesitant moment. His breath, a warming comfort. "Now, find your mom." Silas takes up his perch in the spot Sydney ordered.

Abigail finds her place to my left, tying her flowing auburn hair into a low ponytail and then shaking her hands, like she's stretching and loosening her wrists.

Sydney goes to my right, nodding and taking his stance. He holds his palms out. A green crackling flows through the air, connecting to the wine-colored magic coming from Abigail.

I glance over my shoulder.

Silas mouths, "You got this."

Scanning the contents for what I need, I spot a knife. I take it into my free hand, hovering it above the nearest candle flame until it glows hot. I clench the stone with my thumb and bottom fingers and prick my index finger enough to get the blood I need. I set the knife carefully on the table and push my trickling digit onto the center of the stone.

Immediately activating, the red core lights up, a hissing magic taking hold. It wiggles through my body, the power attaching to me.

Fear hits for a split second, but then I remember Sydney urging me to stay calm, to stay focused.

I close my eyes, thinking only of my mom, to the last time I saw her, so happy, dancing around the house with a renewed vigor. To the temporarily sad mother of the past, to the woman who had once spent hours upon hours tending to her garden and then baking the most outrageous zucchini and chocolate pies. I dig for any memory that might bring me one step closer to her.

Minutes pass, with nothing magical happening, other than the illuminating connection and flowing energy of those around me.

I go deeper, remembering my childhood, my earliest memory. I was young, maybe three or four, and at that point in our lives we spent a lot of time in the yard, running and playing together. But for some reason, it sticks with me to this day, her grabbing my hands, swinging me around in a circle. We were barefoot and laughing, and it was such a perfectly simple moment. The summer sun had begun to set, and the breeze from being spun around was cool and crisp. Her eyes had lit up, and I don't recall ever seeing her smile brighter than that moment.

Tears roll down my cheeks, and disappointment floods through me.

The stone isn't working, or maybe there's nothing to find, because something terrible could have very well happened to her. What if I'm too late? What if I'll never find her?

"What's wrong?" Silas demands from his spot near the door.

"She should have connected to her by now. Get back, don't break the circle," Sydney says.

"Why isn't it doing what it's supposed to do?" I fight through the heavy sadness.

Abigail speaks up. "She could be hidden to the reperio, Willow. This doesn't mean what you think it does. We can keep searching for her."

How can I convince myself that my mom is still out there if all signs point to anything but that? She left a note that she was leaving with Jenny, but Jenny's been long gone for years. Is it possible that she went to find my dad? Why wouldn't she have told me? Kept in contact so I didn't worry? How does any of this make sense?

"Why don't you take a break and try again here in a little while?" Sydney suggests.

I shake my head, gripping the stone in my hand, not allowing a break in the hold.

"Willow, he's right. Give yourself a minute," Silas pleads.

I shut myself off to those around me, whispering the words, "Blood of my blood." Closing my eyes again, I concentrate every fucking brain wave to the man who abandoned us all those years ago, whatever the reasoning may be. If he's alive, maybe finding him will help me find my mother.

But how can I find a man who is nothing but a mystery to

me? Whether it be his name or his face, I have no knowledge of who he is.

Without me taking a peek, a circular wind rushes around me, starting at the floor, weaving its way up, and above my head, whipping violently, almost throwing the rock out of my hand. I clutch it firmly, not giving it the chance to break the connection.

That's when the sign pops into my head, the blue background with a...ripe peach. Georgia's state welcome sign. I focus further and I'm thrown across an interstate, through the winding of back roads, over a bridge. Another marker coming into sight...for...I can barely make it out, but the words fizzle into clarity—Driftwood Beach.

Everything slows down, and a silhouette of a man wanders in the distance, the setting sun casting hues of purple and orange bouncing onto the clouds and water. Large fallen trees clutter the sandy area. I urge my mind to go farther...only a little more.

Two people emerge from the corner of my vision, more delicate figures—women.

I try with all my might, all my magic, everything in me to travel the distance to them, but all too soon, everything comes to an abrupt halt, my eyes flashing open to the altar in front of me.

"What did you see?" Sydney urges.

"I think." I hesitate for a second. "I think I found my father."

# CHAPTER 26

"And you're absolutely sure that's what you saw?" Walker folds his arms over his chest like he's known to do, studying my face heavily with his blueish eyes. His pressed tan shirt wrinkles, and his sleeves ride up.

"It was clear as day." Well, not until it finally came into sight.

He looks around, lost in thought. "The team did get a small lead in the Carolinas, so it's not too far-fetched that she could be in Georgia by now. My concern is whether or not they're on the move." Walker glances at Sydney. "Now, if I'm not mistaken, the reperio can be used only so often?"

Or if they're even together. What if that wasn't my dad or my mom? And who was the third person?

Sydney nods. "That's correct. The stone has to recharge, so to do another location, we'll have to wait about seven to ten days. It won't be until we do one more reading that we can see if their whereabouts change."

A week? Possibly more? I can't wait that long, not with the unknown weighing so heavily.

"Willow, I can imagine you're chomping at the bit to make a move right now." Walker's voice is calm but firm and authoritative. "But I advise you to stay the course. My group is still doing a sweep on the coast, so bear with us while they make their way to that beach. Give them a chance first. You don't know what kind of dangers lie in store for you with your curse. You may think you have a hold on it now, but who's to say the next one won't be more brutal and difficult to handle, especially out on the road." He comes across as a total dad figure, and its equal parts appreciated and frustrating.

"Okay," is all I say, knowing damn well that the period between now and the next reading is going to drag on. But that's all the time I'll allow. I will give them the chance to locate my mother, given what I was able to uncover, but as soon as I'm able to track my father again, I'm going after him myself.

I've waited almost two decades, what's another week? Once the clock has ticked down, I refuse to continue to sit back and do nothing. For now, I'll stomach my pride, give them their last effort, and hope for the best, while preparing for the worst.

"You all right?" Sydney asks from beside me.

I blink, realizing we're in the foyer, walking past the lush garden. I nod. "Mmhm."

"I'll tell you the moment the stone is charged. I promise. I might be able to skim a few days off with the full moon that's coming."

I bob my head again.

He gently but firmly grabs on to my arm, stopping me from moving forward. "Hey."

I take in a breath. "What's up?"

Sydney bites at his lip, his voice low. "Are we okay?"

His question catches me off guard. "Yeah, why?"

He rubs his neck and gazes at the ground. "I...I don't want to lose what we had."

"Some things are more important than that," I repeat the words he spoke to me not that long ago. I'm well aware of the sever between us, but losing him isn't something I'm ready to do either. Our time together has been precious and rare, forging a bond that could never be replicated. "Give it some time, we'll find our way back to each other."

Inching his arm up, he reaches for what I can only imagine is my face.

An instant too soon, Deghan barrels past him. "Shit, another moment I interrupted. I really do have the worst timing."

I smile up at him, his chocolatey golden eyes shining. "We were heading your way." I clutch Sydney's arm, a silent reassurance. "Where's Cam?"

"Showering. He got back from his run a little bit ago." Deghan throws his arm around my shoulder.

Silas's presence calls to me, and I recognize his proximity without any signal other than my body being pulled toward his.

We follow each other into the dining hall, getting some snacks and finding the rest of our friends.

Kyra waves us over and starts talking once we've arrived. "Girl, you will *not* believe what Ian did."

Sitting, I peel the first layer of my orange. "What did he do?"

"He went *streaking...through* the school." She busts out laughing, and it's hard not to notice the way Remi glowers at her. If only she would just make her move already.

I shift my focus to Lillian, her shy smile warming my heart.

We make eye contact, and for once, she doesn't frown. It's like a new page has been turned, ending the chapter of the bad times between us.

Cameron jogs over, taking the seat next to Deghan.

Silas finally joins us, him coming up behind me, his hands on my shoulders, rubbing circles with his thumbs over the sore muscles. I look up at him, the warmth of his company soaking into me.

For a second I lose sight of everything wrong in my life, glancing around at all the people I'm surrounded by. I've been so wrapped up in the negative, the doubting myself for coming here, for thinking I didn't deserve a chance at happiness, or starting fresh, when in reality, this was the best decision I've ever made.

Sure, it's challenging as hell, and life-changing to say the least, but it's what I wanted, what I needed.

To find myself.

To find my people.

To find my place in the world.

Regardless of it all being a work in progress, at least I'm moving toward figuring it all out. One step at a time. One curse at a time.

And I'd be lying if I thought it was going to be smooth sailing from here. Especially with more curses to come, locating my parents, and all the secrets I've still to uncover.

But with a clear mind and a full heart, I'll embark on this journey with open arms. The best part of all?

I won't have to do it alone.

---

Join Willow in the third installment of the Harper Shadow Academy series, Wicked Magic.

# Acknowledgments

**Cursed Magic** was yet another fun and fantastic adventure that I have had the honor of experiencing!

Tiny human, everything I do, I do it for you!

Victoria, I don't know what I would ever do without you.

Kate, your friendship is invaluable.

The folks over at Patreon who help me behind the scenes—I owe a huge thanks to you for your continuous support! Clayton, James, Dustin, Tyler, and Victoria—I appreciate you all tremendously.

The entire RHRA group, your encouragement has helped push this series to what it is!

To the readers of the **Harper Shadow Academy**, I can't thank you enough for joining me and cheering me on to make you more books! Your support is what makes this all possible!

# Also by Luna Pierce

**The Harper Shadow Academy Series**

(Paranormal academy reverse harem)

Hidden Magic

Cursed Magic

Wicked Magic

Ancient Magic

Sacred Magic

Harper Shadow Academy: Complete Box Set

**Falling for the Enemy Series**

(Paranormal reverse harem)

Stolen by Monsters

Fighting for Monsters

Fated to Monsters

**Sinners and Angels Universe**

Broken Like You (Standalone)

Untamed Vixen (Part One)

Villain Era (Part Two)

Wings of a Devil (Standalone novella)

Ruin My Life (Standalone)

London & Archer's Story (Standalone)

# About the Author

**Luna Pierce** is a paranormal and contemporary romance author who loves getting lost in her stories. She brings you tough characters that love fiercely and fight for what's right. Luna loves all things gritty, and even supernatural, especially: witches, vampires, and werewolves.

Join Luna's newsletter to receive updates at:
www.lunapierce.com/subscribe

If you enjoy my books, please consider leaving a review on Amazon, Goodreads, or Bookbub.

Want to chat about the book and tell me the things you liked and disliked about **Cursed Magic**? I'd love to hear from you!

Join the exclusive reader group — Luna Pierce's Paranormal Addicts